'I'm your Chr...

'Excuse me?' Blake...

'I bet you never had a Christmas present like me before.' The woman smiled.

'You're pregnant,' he stated.

'Yes, I'm pregnant. Great work for noticing.'

'Have you come to see me about your pregnancy, Miss McKenzie?'

'It's Dr McKenzie. And I'm your Christmas present.'

'Just explain,' Blake said.

'Your friends Jonas and Emily have organised it all with the hospital board. They're giving you a holiday and I'll take over!'

'It's a very nice idea,' Blake forced out. 'But it's impossible. You can't just take over my Christmas. I see fifty patients a day!'

'Fifty? OK, maybe I can't. But maybe I can share it.'

'What?'

'Well, maybe we could have a Christmas to remember. Together.'

Marion Lennox was born on an Australian dairy farm. She moved on—mostly because the cows weren't interested in her stories! Marion writes Medical Romance™ as well as Tender Romance™. Initially she used a different name for each category, so if you're looking for past books, search also for author Trisha David.

In her non-writing life Marion cares (haphazardly) for her husband, teenagers, dogs, cats, chickens and anyone else who lines up at her dinner table. She fights her rampant garden (she's losing) and her house dust (she's lost). She also travels, which she finds seriously addictive. As a teenager Marion was told she'd never get anywhere reading romance. Now romance is the basis of her stories; her stories allow her to travel, and if ever there was an advertisement for following your dream, she'd be it!

Recent titles by the same author:

A ROYAL PROPOSITION (Tender Romance™)
THE DOCTORS' BABY* (Medical Romance™)
ADOPTED: TWINS!* (Tender Romance™)
THEIR BABY BARGAIN* (Tender Romance™)

*Parents Wanted Quartet

DR BLAKE'S ANGEL

BY
MARION LENNOX

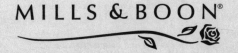

MILLS & BOON®

First published in Great Britain 2002
Harlequin Mills & Boon Limited,
Eton House, 18-24 Paradise Road, Richmond, Surrey TW9 1SR

© Marion Lennox 2002

ISBN 0 263 83108 6

Set in Times Roman 10½ on 11 pt.
03-1202-51985

Printed and bound in Spain
by Litografia Rosés, S.A., Barcelona

CHAPTER ONE

'I'M NOT a patient. I'm your Christmas present.'

Right...

The woman had glossy, copper-red hair. She was wearing purple patchwork overalls, a pink T-shirt and pink flowery sandals. She was also heavily pregnant.

Dr Blake Sutherland still had urgent house calls to do. He'd promised Grace Mayne he'd visit her tonight and the elderly fisherwoman was already waiting. He'd been up since dawn, he was exhausted and now he had a nutcase on his hands.

'Excuse me?'

'I bet you've never had a Christmas present like me.' The woman's bright smile exuded happiness.

Who on earth was she? Blake didn't have a clue. She'd arrived an hour ago, settled to wait for his last afternoon appointment and had been placidly reading old copies of *Rich and Famous* until he'd found time to see her.

His Christmas present...

On reflection, he decided to ignore what she'd said and try again. 'You're pregnant.' He sat back and did a slow assessment. She was at least seven months, he guessed, or maybe more. She was glowing with the health most women found in late stages of pregnancy, and she looked...lovely?

Lovely was as good a way as any to describe her, he decided as he took in her startling appearance. Her riot of copper curls was close cropped but not enough to stop the rioting. Her freckled face was enhanced by huge green eyes, and she had the most gorgeous smile...

Oh, for heaven's sake! Ignore the smile. She also had a problem or she wouldn't be here.

'Yes, I'm pregnant. Great work for noticing.' She chuckled. It was a nice, throaty chuckle that went beautifully with her eyes. 'Em said you were a brilliant doctor, and you've just proved it. Pregnant, hey?' She patted her tummy. 'Well, well. Who'd have guessed it?'

He had the grace to smile. 'I'm sorry, but—'

'I guess since I'm pregnant you have two gifts for the price of one—but maybe the outer package is the only useful bit. That's me.'

She was a nutcase! But she *was* pregnant and she may well have medical needs. He needed to step warily. The worst medical mistakes were made when doctors were tired, and he didn't intend to toss her out unchecked because she was a bit unbalanced.

'Have you come to see me about your pregnancy?' He glanced at her naked ring finger and took a punt. 'Miss…' Another glance to the card his receptionist had given him. 'Miss McKenzie.'

'It's Dr McKenzie,' she told him. 'Or Nell if you prefer.' Her smile deepened and she held out her hand in greeting. Dazed, he took it. 'Nell's better. Dr McKenzie always makes me feel like someone's talking to my grandfather.'

Her hand was warm and firm. His hand was shaken and released and that was how he felt. Shaken.

This conversation was way out of line, he decided. He didn't have a clue what was going on. 'Miss… Doctor…'

'Hey, you *are* exhausted,' she said, on a note of discovery. 'Emily and Jonas told me you were. They said you really, really needed me, and after an hour in your waiting room I'm starting to see that they're right.'

'Look, Miss—'

'Doctor,' she reminded him, and she smiled again. It was *some* smile. It was a smile that lit parts of the room he hadn't even known were dark.

He sat back and let his tired eyes assess her. She really was wearing the most amazing outfit. She looked exceedingly cute, he decided. And her red hair gleamed. Actually, all of her gleamed! She sort of beamed all over...

'Doctor, then.' He continued his visual assessment but his mind was working overtime.

She was right, he thought. He was exhausted. This town had far too much work for one doctor and the weeks before Christmas had seen things go haywire. It was the start of the silly season, and whatever happened in the town, the consequences usually ended up here. In his surgery.

That included barmy pregnant ladies who said they were doctors...

'Can I ask—?'

'I think you should.' She rested her hands lightly on her very pregnant tummy. 'Ask away. Or I can explain by myself if you'd rather.'

'Go ahead,' he said faintly, and her smile deepened.

'You promise not to rope me into a strait-jacket?'

'I promise no such thing.' Her smile was infectious. Somehow he found the corners of his mouth twitching in response. 'But I'll listen.'

That was better! Nell settled further back into her chair and relaxed. He seemed nice, she thought. And he was younger than she'd expected. Jonas and Emily had described him as best they could but it had hardly been a comprehensive description.

'Blake's in his mid-thirties,' Em had told her. 'He's got the most gorgeous gold-brown hair and smily brown eyes. Creasy eyes, if you know what I mean. Nice. They're tired creased as well as laughter creased but I guess you'd expect that after what he's gone through. And what he's going through. His life's all medicine. Work, work and more work. Except his marathon running—though how he finds the time to fit that in is anyone's guess.'

Emily had sighed as she'd described him. 'You'll like him, Nell. You must. Anyone would. It's a damned shame...' She'd hauled herself back on track. 'No matter.

But what else? Oh, he's tall. Over six feet. He's taller than Jonas.'

'Oh, for heaven's sake...' Jonas had interrupted then, cutting across his wife with good humour. 'Nell wants a medical description—not the sort of description you'd find in the lonely hearts column.' Jonas had grimaced his disgust, and Nell had grinned.

'OK, Jonas. What would you tell me about him?'

'He's a great guy. He likes beer.'

'Gee, that's useful,' Nell retorted, and both the women had chuckled.

'Well, he's a really talented surgeon,' Jonas told her, in a valiant attempt to fill in the bits his wife had left out. 'His training is in vascular as well as general surgery, so Sandy Ridge is lucky to have him. He's one caring doctor, with far more skills than the normal country doctor possesses. But Em's right. He drives himself into the ground.'

'Which is where you come in,' Em had added.

Which was where Nell came in. She'd gone to visit her friends and she'd ended up here.

So now Nell faced Blake Sutherland across the desk and she knew what she had to say. 'It's as I told you,' she said blandly. 'I'm your Christmas present. Take me or leave me, but I'm here, to use as you will.'

Blake Sutherland was not often flummoxed, but he was flummoxed now. And he was also so tired that he was having trouble understanding what was in front of him.

Sandy Ridge was an isolated medical community. Thirty miles to the north, the marriage of Jonas Lunn and Emily Mainwaring had given Bay Beach good medical cover, and his two friends gave him his only time off, but it wasn't enough.

That was the way he liked it, he'd told himself over and over through the two years he'd been here. He liked being a country doctor, and he liked being on his own. It was just every so often that he felt snowed under.

Like now. Like when he had the Christmas rush and a crazy pregnant stranger to cope with, and too many house calls after that.

'You'd better explain a bit more,' he managed, and Nell's smile softened into sympathy.

'Can I get you a cup of tea while I do?'

A cup of tea? She'd booked in as his patient and *she* was offering *him* cups of tea?

'Thank you, but no.'

'You look like you need it.'

What he needed was to get out of here. He needed to do his house calls, see Grace Mayne and then he needed to sleep—for about a hundred years!

'Can you just tell me what the problem is, and let me get on with my day?' he said wearily. 'Have you filled in a new patient summary?' He lifted a form and held it up without hope. Marion should have insisted she fill it out. He had no idea why she hadn't.

'Fill out a form when I could read ancient copies of *Rich and Famous* magazine?' Nell grinned. 'Why would I do that? I've been learning all about Madonna's love life, and very interesting it is, too. Much more gripping than anything I could write on a stupid form. And I'm not a new patient.'

'Then would you mind telling me what the heck you are?'

'I'm trying,' she complained. 'But you keep interrupting. I'm your Christmas present.'

'My Christmas present.'

'Yes.'

Blake sat back and gazed at this extraordinary purple and pink vision and he had trouble convincing himself he wasn't hallucinating.

'You're not gift-wrapped,' he said cautiously, and received a grin for his pains.

'That's the trouble with being so pregnant. It's hard to find enough wrapping paper.' She hesitated. 'You don't think we could find a pub where we could talk about this, do you?'

'Why do we need a pub?'

'It's just… Maybe we need a Christmas tree and some mistletoe and a bit more atmosphere.'

'Just explain.' It was a growl but he was at the end of his tether.

And she realised it. Nell spread her hands and she smiled across the desk at him—her very nicest smile.

'It's simple,' she told him. 'Your friends, Jonas and Emily, the doctors at Bay Beach…'

'I know who Jonas and Emily are.'

'Then you'll also know that they're very grateful to you for giving them time off when they need it. But you won't reciprocate, and with the sudden popularity of Sandy Ridge as a tourist destination your workload's become huge. So now…'

'So now?'

'They're repaying the favour. They're giving you a holiday. Four weeks, to be precise. Jonas was hoping to come himself but, with Robby recovering from his latest skin graft and another baby on the way, they don't want to leave each other over Christmas. When I said I was coming here…'

'You were coming here?' He was clutching at straws.

'Sandy Ridge is my home,' she told him. His look of incredulity seemed to annoy her. 'I might not have lived here for ten years, but I own the house out on the bluff. It's my home now. Or it will be soon. I intend to do it up and live in it.'

'But—'

'Yeah, there's the but,' she acknowledged. 'The place is a mess. I need to put a landmine under it to clear out the junk, and I need a base while I do it. That's where you come in. I'm only seven months pregnant so I'm good for at least another four weeks' work. Em said you needed someone now, so she and Jonas organised with your hospital board to pay me locum wages for four weeks. That means you, Dr Sutherland, can take yourself off for a Christmas holiday, and leave me with your responsibilities. All of them.'

To say he was flabbergasted would be an understatement. To walk away for four weeks...

No.

'The thing's impossible. I don't know what Jonas and Emily are thinking of.'

'They're thinking of you.'

'I can't go away.'

'Why not?' She smiled at him and her wide eyes were innocent. 'I'm very well qualified. Ring Sydney Central and they'll tell you. I worked with Jonas before he was married—that's how we met.' She arched her eyebrows, knowing before she said it that her next statement was hardly likely to be believed. 'In fact, I'm a very responsible doctor. Until last week I was in charge of Sydney Central Emergency.'

This was crazier and crazier. 'So why aren't you now?'

'In case you hadn't noticed, I'm a little bit pregnant.' She was talking to him as if he was stupid, and that was how he felt. 'I'm moving on. The new registrar can start work now, and Jonas said you needed me.' She smiled. 'So I came. If I'd left it much longer I could have dropped my bundle on your doorstep, and I wouldn't be much use to you with a baby in arms. Or not for a while.'

Blake took a deep breath. 'So let me get this straight. You've quit your job early specifically so you can give me four weeks' leave?'

'That's right.'

'And you're just going to walk in here and take over?'

'That's the plan.'

He shook his head in disbelief. 'I can't just walk out.'

'I expect it'll take a day or two to hand over.'

'You couldn't do it.'

'Don't be ridiculous,' she retorted. 'If you can cope with the medical needs of the town, I don't see why I can't.'

'Hell!'

'Why is it hell?' It was a polite enquiry—nothing more.

'You don't know anybody.'

She had an answer to that, too. 'That's where you're wrong. I lived here for the first seventeen years of my life so I imagine I know more people in the district than you do.'

He shook his head again, trying to clear the fog of weariness and confusion. 'Jonas and Em have paid you?' It came out an incredulous croak and she smiled.

'And the hospital board. Yes, indeed. An obscene amount.' She chuckled. 'No more than I'm worth, of course, but an obscene amount for all that.' She made her lips prim. 'I expect you'll have to write them a very nice thank-you note.'

He stared at her, baffled. 'You have it all sorted.'

'Of course.'

'The fact that you're pregnant didn't enter your calculations as something that needs to be factored in?'

'I'm a very fit pregnant doctor,' she told him.

Silence.

'The idea's stupid,' he said at last, and she shook her head.

'It's not stupid at all. Your hospital board have approved it. They're the ones who employ me—not you. I don't see you have much choice.'

He thought it through. On the surface it seemed fine. Only... 'Do you have any idea how many patients I see in a day?'

'I guess...a lot?'

'I've seen fifty today.'

'Fifty.' For the first time, her confidence ebbed a little. 'Fifty!'

'That's not including hospital rounds, and not including house calls. It's peak holiday season and I'm snowed under.

I started at six this morning, I don't expect to be finished before eleven and if I'm unlucky—and I'm nearly always unlucky—there'll be calls out during the night.'

'Good grief!'

'If you took it on—'

'I must.' She might be dismayed but she was still game. 'I made a bargain.'

'If you took it on you'd drive your blood pressure sky high. You'd give yourself eclampsia and I'd have a dead baby—and maybe even a dead mother on my hands. You think I want that?'

'Hey, that's a bit extreme.'

'Go home, Dr McKenzie,' Blake said wearily. He raked his hand through his hair. It verged on being too long, Nell thought inconsequentially, but, then, why shouldn't it be long? He had the loveliest hair. It was sort of sun-bleached brown with streaks of frost, and it was thick and curling. His strongly boned face, his tanned skin and deep brown eyes made him almost stunningly good-looking.

Oh, for heaven's sake! What was she thinking of? Get a grip! she told herself. Focus on what's important.

'Home's here,' she said softly, and watched as his startled gaze met hers.

'What do you mean?'

'I mean I've moved here. For ever. I want to have my baby here.'

'You want to deliver your baby in Sandy Ridge?' The idea was ridiculous. People didn't come to Sandy Ridge to have their babies. They left Sandy Ridge to have babies. With only one doctor, maternity was frankly dangerous.

He was shocked into saying the first thing that came into his head, and as soon as he said it he knew it wasn't wise, but it came out anyway. 'And the baby's father? What does he think of you moving here?'

She glared at that. Then her eyes fell to his hand. To a gold band on his ring finger.

'And your wife?' She used the same tone he'd used on

her, and it was frankly accusing. Their eyes locked across the desk, anger meeting anger. 'What does your wife think of you working yourself into the ground? Or isn't your personal life any of my business? OK, Dr Sutherland.' Her glare grew angrier. 'You tell me yours and I'll tell you mine.'

His gaze fell first. '*Touché*,' he said lightly, but she knew the word wasn't meant lightly at all. He'd been touched on the raw.

As had she. Damn, she wasn't going to feel sorry for the man. Or for herself. She was here to take over his responsibilities for a month and then get out of his life. But...

'How many patients a day did you say?' she asked faintly, and his mouth curved into the beginnings of a smile.

'Fifty.'

It gave her pause. 'I don't think I can—'

'I don't think you can either.' He rose. 'So it was a very nice idea, from you and from Jonas and Emily and the hospital board. But it's impractical and impossible. I'll ring them and thank them—as I thank you—but I think we should leave it at that. Don't you?'

'No.'

'No?'

'I told Jonas and Emily that I'd give you a decent Christmas.'

'And I've said it's impossible. You can't take over my Christmas.'

'No,' she said slowly, and her chin jutted into a look of sheer stubbornness. 'OK. Maybe I can't. But maybe I can share it.'

'What?'

'Maybe somehow we could have a Christmas to remember. Together.'

Nell wouldn't be budged. No matter how many arguments he raised, she countered them.

'You need a rest. You know you do.'

'Yes, but—'

'You know very well that a tired doctor is a dangerous doctor.'

'I can—'

'You can't. No one can. When you're tired, your judgement's impaired. That's why Jonas and Emily are worried about you.'

'Did they say my judgement was impaired?'

'Not yet. But it will be.'

'For heaven's sake, this is ridiculous.'

'What's ridiculous,' she said serenely, 'is you continuing to argue with me.'

'I don't even know you,' he threw at her, goaded. 'You walk in here like some outlandish—'

And that had been the wrong thing to say!

'You don't like my overalls?' She stood up, her eyes flashing fire. 'You don't like my gorgeous patchwork overalls? And you're judging me on them? How dare you? Of all the intolerant, prejudiced, male chauvinist—'

'I didn't say anything about your overalls,' he said weakly, but she stalked around the desk and advanced on him.

'Outlandish! What about me is outlandish except for my overalls?'

'Your temper?' he tried.

That brought her up short. She stopped a foot away from Blake and she glared.

'You *meant* my overalls.'

'They're…they're wonderful.'

'I made them myself.'

'Like I said—'

'They're wonderful,' she agreed, her eyes narrowing. 'Not outlandish.'

'I…not outlandish.'

'You're not colour prejudiced?'

'I like pink. And purple…'

'That's enough. There's no reason to go overboard.' Nell glared some more. 'Do we have a deal, Dr Sutherland, or do I go to the medical board and say you won't employ me because of stupid prejudices about pregnancy and patchwork pants?'

'I'm not employing you.'

'No. The hospital board is. And they already have. So if I'm now unemployed then I've been sacked and you're the one that's doing it. So I'm right. Prejudice...'

'I'm not prejudiced.'

'You want a quiet Christmas?'

'Yes.' How would he get a quiet Christmas if this virago was in town?

'Then do what we want. Let me share your load. Let me take on as much as I can, while you enjoy mince pies and mistletoe to the max.'

'I can't.' He took a deep breath. 'Look. Miss McKenzie—'

'Doctor!' It was an angry snap. 'Think it through. Think of what you're refusing.'

He took another breath, but still she glared at him. Her anger gave him pause. It made him stop and count to ten...

And counting to ten helped. It did give him time to think.

'Um...' he said, and she homed right in on it.

'Yes?'

She was deadly serious, he saw. She really was intending to live in the place. 'Maybe you could just do morning clinics for a bit,' he said weakly. That might get her out of his hair.

And maybe it'd even be a good idea.

It was a generous offer Jonas and Em had made. So maybe he should accept. If this woman could take on his morning work then he'd have only a normal day's work left to do himself.

She considered what he'd said and her anger faded. A little. 'It's a start,' she said grudgingly, sinking back into her chair and watching him across the desk. 'But I've been paid to work.' She brightened. 'I can take every second night's house calls.'

He bit his lip. 'You can't. The emergency calls are switched through to my house. It'd be too much trouble to change the system just for a month.'

'We wouldn't need to change the system.'

'Why not?'

'Because Em told me the situation here is the same as the one at Bay Beach,' she said sweetly. 'The hospital has the doctor's residence attached and it has four bedrooms. They were built at the same optimistic time—when hospital boards imagined doctors might *like* becoming country practitioners in remote areas. So, that's a bedroom for you, there's one for me, there's one for Ernest and there's one left for whoever wants to drop in.'

Ernest? Who was Ernest? Another child? A partner?

Blake didn't want to know. It was irrelevant. 'You can't stay with me.'

'Why ever not?' Her eyes widened in enquiry. 'The doctors' residence is supposed to be for doctors—isn't it? It's designed for up to four doctors. There's two here. Me and you.'

'Yes, but—'

'And my house is unlivable. That's one of the reasons I agreed to do this locum.'

'Miss McKenzie—'

'It's Dr McKenzie,' she said sweetly. 'And the board has already given me permission to move in with you. You know, you're going to have to get used to it. And...you really don't want to refuse.'

He looked across the desk and met her eyes. She'd calmed down, he realised. The laughter and temper and over-the-top threats had died. What was left was understanding. And sympathy.

And something more?

Something he didn't understand.

But he didn't want this woman in his house. He didn't want *anyone* in his house.

He didn't want anyone in his life!

And who was Ernest?

He was saved by the waiting-room bell. Marion, his receptionist, had ushered Nell into his surgery but with the last patient safely with Blake, she'd felt free to leave, so there was no one out there to see what the problem was.

'I need to see who this is.'

She glowered. 'There's no need to sound pleased. We haven't come to an arrangement.'

'Afterwards,' he told her, and opened the door with real relief.

CHAPTER TWO

As A rescuing angel, Ethel Norris didn't quite make the grade.

She was a massive woman, weighing close to twenty stone. Normally well groomed and cheerful, she was anything but well groomed now. Her clothes were soiled. Her mass of grey curls looked as if it hadn't been brushed since she'd climbed out of bed this morning and her cheeks were grubby with tearstains. She looked up as Blake entered the reception area, and the look she gave him said it was the end of her world.

'Oh, Dr Sutherland. Dr Sutherland...' She put her face in her hands and sobbed as if her heart were breaking.

'Hey...Ethel.' He guided her to a chair and pushed her into it, then knelt before her and pulled her hands away from her face. 'What is it?' His eyes were on hers. He was totally focussed on her distress, unaware that Nell had followed him to the door and was watching.

'I can't... I couldn't...'

'You couldn't what?'

'I broke.' She took a ragged gasp. 'And I've been doing so well. I've lost four stone and you were so pleased with me. My clothes have been getting looser and looser, and then all of a sudden I couldn't go on. I dunno. I sort of snapped. I went out and bought everything I could find. Ice cream. Biscuits...' She took a searing gulp. 'Not just one. Tubs and tubs of ice cream. Packets and packets of biscuits. I've stuffed myself stupid, and I've been sick but not sick enough. I'll have put all my weight back on and I can't bear it.'

'Ethel, you can't have put it all back on.'

'I have.' It was a wail of agony.

'How long have you been dieting?' Nell's voice cut across both of them.

Blake flashed her a look of annoyance but Nell seemed unconcerned. In fact, she appeared not to even notice.

'You must have been dieting for ever to lose four stone,' she said in a voice of awe. 'That's fantastic.'

Ethel looked up at her, her attention caught. Well, how could it not be caught by purple patchwork?

'Don't mind me. I'm just another doctor,' Nell told her blithely. 'I'm Dr Sutherland's new associate. But losing four stone. Wow!'

'I haven't—'

'How long have you been dieting?'

'Six months.'

'And this is the first time you've cracked?' Nell's voice remained awed. 'Six months of solid dieting! I never heard of such a thing. That's fantastic.'

'But now I've ruined it.'

'How have you ruined it?' Nell's eyes took in the vastness of the woman's figure, and her sharp intelligence was working overtime. Ethel must have had a serious eating disorder over many years to account for so much weight. 'It's my guess that eating a few tubs of ice cream wasn't a rare occurrence before you started dieting,' she said softly. 'You did it often—right?'

'Yes. But—'

'But now you've had a day off your diet.'

'I wasn't just off my diet.' The woman wailed. 'I binged.'

'Well, I don't blame you,' Nell said stoutly. 'If I'd lost four stone in six months then I'd binge, too.'

'Dr McKenzie.' Blake was glaring at her. This was his patient. She had no business butting in.

'Yes, Dr Sutherland?' She gave him her sweetest smile. 'Am I saying what you were about to say? I'm sure I am.

I understand all about diets. I've been on 'em ever since I was a kid.'

'You?' the woman whispered, and Nell chuckled.

'Yeah, well, I'm not on one now. As you see, I'm a bit pregnant and it'd be bad for baby. But as soon as I stop breastfeeding I'll be back to dieting. I just have to look at a tub of ice cream and I gain a midriff.'

'But nothing like me.'

'But not like you,' Nell agreed. 'I'd imagine you and Dr Sutherland have talked about the underlying problems— why you got so big in the first place.'

'Yes, but—'

'But nothing.' Nell crossed to Blake's side. She stooped and elbowed him aside. 'Dr Sutherland, this is women's business.'

He glowered. 'How can it be women's business?'

'Have you ever dieted?' She looked up and down at his long, lean frame. 'Marathon man.'

He was taken aback. 'No.'

'There you go, then.' Another sweet smile. Then she turned back to Ethel. 'You know, losing the amount of weight you need to lose to be healthy is going to take a couple of years.'

'I know that. That's why it's so terrible…'

'That you broke? No. That's why it's understandable. And there's no way you'll have gained four stone in a one-day binge. You won't have come close.' Nell smiled. 'You know, I'm watching my weight while I'm pregnant, but I can't do it all the time. I'd go stark staring mad. So I give myself days off.'

'Days off?'

'Like Christmas.' Nell's voice was totally serious now. She had eye contact with Ethel and she wasn't letting go. Woman to woman. 'Christmas is in two weeks. I can last until then, but I intend to eat way too much on Christmas Day. Far too much. Then on Boxing Day I'll think how much I enjoyed it and get on with being sensible.'

'But—'

'But there's lots more time to go before you hit an ideal weight,' Nell agreed. 'More so for you than for me, but eating sensibly is a lifetime thing for all of us. So I won't make it impossible for myself again. I'll promise myself a day off from being sensible on New Year's Day. Then January fourteenth is my cocker spaniel's birthday so that's a day off, too. Because how can he celebrate alone? After that… Well, no one can diet on January twenty-sixth. That's Australia Day, and it wouldn't be patriotic! And in February… I'll think of something to celebrate. There's bound to be a reason if I put my mind to it.'

The woman caught her breath. Her tears had been arrested. Nell had her fascinated, and Ethel gazed at her purple midriff in awe. 'You might…you might have your baby. In February, I mean.'

'So I might,' Nell said with aplomb, appearing exceedingly pleased. 'There you go, then. There's no need to circle the calendar for that one. It's a ready-made celebration.'

'It sounds crazy.'

Nell shook her head. 'No. It sounds logical. You need to see some light at the end of the tunnel. You can't keep losing weight for years without breaks, and those breaks need to be planned well ahead or you'll crack again.'

'But Dr Sutherland says—'

'Does Dr Sutherland disagree?' She swung around to face him, and the look she gave him was determined. 'Surely not? Do you, Dr Sutherland?'

He managed to rise to the occasion. Somehow. 'Days off seem a very good idea to me,' he said, and she grinned.

'See? We have consensus.' She turned back to Ethel. 'OK, what are you planning for Christmas dinner?'

'I hadn't thought about it. Maybe a fillet of fish.'

'A lone fish fillet for Christmas dinner?' Nell sounded appalled. 'Oh, you poor dear, no wonder you binged. You're absolutely forgiven and then some. Isn't she, Dr Sutherland?'

Blake could only gaze at her in astonishment. And agree. There was nowhere else to go. 'Um…yes.'

'You need turkey and roast potatoes and cranberry sauce and pudding,' Nell said solidly. 'With brandy cream. Not brandy butter. Trust me. I'm an expert on this one. You can't get enough brandy into brandy butter. I know this fantastic recipe for brandy cream, where's it's so alcoholic no one ends up knowing who's pulled which end of the cracker. I'll write it out for you if you like.'

'But—'

'No buts. I'm sick of buts. You're ordered to eat as much as you like on Christmas Day.' Nell's smile softened. 'And I'll bet that, having given yourself permission to eat as much as you like, and with no guilt attached, you won't eat yourself sick. You'll just enjoy your food very much indeed. Then, at the end of the day you give the remains of your pudding to an elderly aunt or the town drunk—or even a very appreciative dog. My cocker spaniel will volunteer if no one else comes forward. You drink the rest of your brandy cream as a nightcap, you wish yourself a merry goodnight—and then you go back to dieting the next day. How easy's that? It'll work. No sweat.'

Ethel looked wildly at Blake. 'Will it?'

But Blake was smiling. 'I don't see why not,' he told her. He took a deep breath. It took a big man to admit he was wrong but maybe… 'Maybe the diet sheet we put you on was a bit harsh long term,' he told her. 'Maybe Dr McKenzie is right.'

'Record this for posterity,' Nell said, mock-stunned, and Ethel even managed a chuckle.

She looked at the pair of them, and she smiled. 'You…you will give me that recipe for brandy cream?'

'Hand over a prescription form,' Nell ordered Blake. 'The lady needs urgent medication. I'll write it up for her now. And, Ethel…'

'Yes?'

'If you love cooking and you want to cook more than

you and your family can eat, then think about offering treats to the nursing home or to the hospital. Or even me!' She chuckled. 'Just don't give this prescription to the pharmacist. He'll think Dr Sutherland's barmy.'

'I think you're both barmy,' Ethel said softly, and for the first time her face relaxed. 'You've made me feel so much better.'

'Punishing yourself is the pits,' Nell said strongly. 'Heck, Ethel, the outside world criticises enough—there's no good to be gained by criticising yourself. And if you've lost four stone you have so much to be proud of.'

'Thank you.' Ethel sighed and rose ponderously to her feet. She looked Nell up and down, really seeing her for the first time. Then she cast an uncertain glance at Blake, and another at Nell. 'Do I know you?'

'I'm Nell McKenzie. My grandparents owned the place out on the bluff.'

'Nell McKenzie!' The woman seemed stunned. 'Well, I never. You've changed so much. And… Did you say you were Dr Sutherland's new associate?'

'That's right.' Nell beamed at Blake, defying him to deny it.

But Ethel was off on the next track. 'They're amazing overalls you're wearing.'

'They are, aren't they?'

'They look as if they're made from a quilt.'

'Funny you should say that,' Nell told her. 'They are. From a king-sized quilt.'

'You cut up a quilt to make overalls?' Ethel's voice took on a horror that said she was a patchworker from way back and Nell had just committed a crime somewhere up there with murder. 'You're joking!'

'No.'

'But why on earth?'

'I needed overalls much more than I needed a king-sized quilt,' Nell said in a tone which stated that no more ques-

tions were welcome on this score. 'Enough of that. OK?
Let's get this prescription written and get Christmas on the
road.'

Blake left her writing her brandy-cream script and made a
fast phone call. Was she really who she said she was?

She said she'd come from Emily and Jonas but he didn't
want to ring his friends yet. He knew the surgical registrar
at Sydney Central. It took five minutes to page Daniel, but
he came through with the goods straight away.

'Nell McKenzie? Of course I know her. She's the best
damned doctor we've had in Emergency for a long time
and we're going to miss her badly. There's been pressure
on her to put her baby in child care here and keep on
working.'

'Why doesn't she?'

'Who knows?' Daniel hesitated. 'But it'd be a hard job.
Emergency's relentless, and who knows how much support
she has? She's kept her private life very much to herself.
She's such a mousy little thing that—'

Mousy little thing!' Blake sat back in his chair at that,
and frowned. 'We must have the wrong woman.'

'Five four-ish high, freckles, red hair hauled back like
she's ashamed of it?'

'There are similarities, but—'

'Oh, she's not mousy around patients,' Daniel told him.
'She's extremely competent and decisive and very, very
kind. The patients love her. But…you know…she's sort of
self-effacing. We didn't even know she had a boyfriend or
a husband, and we were stunned when she announced she
was pregnant. The nurses had a running joke about im-
maculate conception.'

'Good grief.'

'But if she's turned up at Sandy Ridge… Hell, Blake,
don't look a gift horse in the mouth. If you have Nell
McKenzie wanting to work with you, then you hang onto
her with everything you have. She's worth her weight in
gold.'

*   *   *

A real little work horse. Blake came back out to Reception as Nell waved goodbye to Ethel and gazed at her incredulously. Anything less like a work horse he had yet to meet.

But she was here. She was another doctor and he really was overworked.

Who was Ernest?

It couldn't matter.

'All right,' he managed. 'All right.'

'All right what?'

'All right, you can stay.'

Her smile flashed back into her eyes. 'Gee, that's nice of you—and so gracious.'

He glowered. She had him unnerved. 'I can cope on my own.'

'I'm sure you can.' she told him. 'But you'll crack eventually. You can't go on working at this pace for ever.'

'I have for two years.'

'And it's getting to you.'

'It's *not* getting to me.'

'OK, it's not getting to you,' she agreed blithely, and grinned again. 'You're coping magnificently. All's well with the world and I'm doomed to spend four weeks being a pest. But that's my fate, Dr Sutherland. I know my place in life. Pest *extraordinaire*. So can we get on with it?'

He was having trouble keeping up with her. 'What—now?'

'Take me to where I'm going to live,' she told him, smiling sweetly. 'Take me to the doctors' quarters and then we'll get on with me being your Christmas present.'

The doctors' quarters were not to Nell McKenzie's liking. She took one step through the door and stopped short.

'How long did you say you've been living here?' she asked in stunned amazement, and Blake gazed around defensively.

'Two years. It's not so bad.'

'It's awful.'

'Gee, thanks. If I go into your home, would you be happy if I said it was awful?'

'I'd hope someone would point it out if it was this bad.'

'It's not *this bad*.'

'It's worse.' She stared around the starkly furnished apartment in distaste.

OK, it wasn't very good, Blake admitted. The last doctor at Sandy Ridge—Chris Maitland—had lived offsite. When Blake had taken over from Chris two years ago, the doctors' quarters had contained a stark laminex table with four vinyl chairs, a vinyl couch and a plain bedstead in each room. Oh, and one black and white television. There had been nothing more, and Blake had never had the time or the inclination to turn the place into something else.

'You can't live here all the time,' Nell breathed, and Blake found himself getting more and more annoyed.

'Of course I do. Where else would I go?'

'Oh, for heaven's sake...' She stalked over and hauled open the bedroom doors one after the other. The only difference between his bedroom and the others was that Blake's bed was made up and there was a pile of medical journals on the floor. 'Very cosy,' she retorted. She swivelled back to face him. 'Where's your Christmas tree?'

'Why would I need a Christmas tree?'

Why indeed? They gazed at each other, eyes locked, and her gaze was accusatory. Like he'd personally shot Santa Claus!

This time he was saved by his beeper. He looked at the little screen and he sighed. He was needed. It was more work—of course—but his sigh was a sigh of relief.

'I need to go.'

'Of course you need to go,' Nell said cordially. 'I would too if I stayed in this dump.'

'You asked to live here.'

'Nobody lives here. People *stay* here. There's a difference. You don't *live* on torn green vinyl dining chairs and ugly grey linoleum. You exist.'

'I'm leaving,' he told her. 'I have a patient in hospital who has heart problems, and then I have house calls to make. Make yourself comfortable.'

'Comfortable? Humph! Ernest will hate this place.'

Who the hell was Ernest? He didn't have time to find out. 'Well, ring Jonas and Em and complain about your working conditions,' he said with asperity. 'I'm sure the three of you can work it out. You're all so good at organising.'

'We are at that.'

He cast her a last, long, dubious look. There were schemes going on behind those sea-green eyes. He could feel their vibes from where he was.

Who was Ernest?

'Don't do anything. Just unpack.'

'And I'll make myself comfortable,' she said. 'It's what all guests do.'

'Don't!'

'Go, Dr Sutherland,' she said cheerfully. 'Go and doctor to those who need doctoring. Leave me to my own devices.'

He didn't have a choice. He left.

By the time Blake reached Casualty, Harriet Walsingham's heart had decided to behave.

'Though it gave me quite a scare, Doctor,' she said, sitting up and crossing her ankles primly on the ambulance trolley. 'I came over all funny, I did.'

'Then you can lie straight down again in case you come over all funny again,' he told her, pressing her gently back on the pillows and moving his stethoscope into position. 'What exactly happened?'

'She was out cold on the kitchen floor,' one of the ambulance officers told him, and Blake looked a question at the younger of the two men. If something was grey, Henry painted it black.

'Bob?'

'She wasn't unconscious,' Bob told him truthfully. 'She was just gasping like a fish out of water and she'd managed to grab the phone and call us.'

'It's got to be angina pectoris,' Henry told him triumphantly. 'Like I told you when we called. That's what it'll be. Won't it, Doc?'

'Possibly.' Not for the first time Blake thought longingly of big cities and fully trained paramedics. Henry was the local postman and Bob ran the menswear store. For them, a call for the ambulance meant major excitement in otherwise humdrum lives.

If only they wouldn't act like would-be doctors, he thought. Half the patients who arrived at the hospital via ambulance had been given an amateur diagnosis on the way, and sometimes it scared the pants off them.

'What's angina pectoris?' Luckily, Harriet wasn't one to let big words scare her. She was just like the ambulance officers—seemingly grateful for such an interesting event to disrupt her mundane existence. She gave a delicious shiver. 'Is it dangerous?' She really was feeling better.

'It's when your heart muscle is starved for oxygen,' Blake told her. 'But by itself it's not dangerous. Shush for a minute while I listen.'

They all shushed. For about ten seconds. Then…

'Can I have our new Dr McKenzie look after me?' Harriet enquired. 'No offence, Dr Blake, but I've always fancied a lady doctor, and she sounds lovely. I remember her when she was a teenager. She was such a sweet little thing, but so quiet.'

Our new Dr McKenzie… 'How did you know about Nell?'

'It's all over town,' Harriet told him. 'It's so exciting. Lorna is on the hospital board and she told me in strictest confidence. She said no one was allowed to say anything until today because they wanted to surprise you. You must be so pleased. Isn't it the best Christmas present?'

He took a deep breath. Was the whole town in on this? 'Harriet, be quiet.'

'But it *is* exciting.'

'I'll sedate you if you don't shut up,' he told her. Angina might be a minor problem, but it could also be a symptom of something major. 'Let's get you admitted and get an ECG done.' He glanced up at the ambulancemen. 'Thanks, boys.'

'Think nothing of it.' The men moved reluctantly off and then stopped. There was clearly something bothering them. 'How are we going to get to meet our new doctor, then?' Bob asked. He hesitated. 'Shouldn't there be some sort of function to welcome her back? So she can get to know people like us? Except for her grandma's funeral it's been over ten years since she was home. We'd hardly recognise her.'

'She's only here for four weeks.'

Bob shook his head. 'Lorna says it might be for longer. If the town's nice to her—for a change—and if she settles here after the bub's born, then she might stay.'

'And if she likes you, Dr Blake.' Harriet giggled. 'Not that she couldn't.'

Blake took a deep breath. This was getting out of hand. A welcome party? 'We're hardly likely to find any comers for a welcome party in the weeks before Christmas.'

'But it's Nell McKenzie,' Bob said, as if that made everything different.

'You'll have to explain.'

'The town feels bad about Nell McKenzie,' Harriet told him. 'And in a way maybe we should. No one ever did anything.'

'We couldn't,' Henry retorted. 'We weren't allowed to.'

'No, but she was such a little thing. And they were so awful.'

'Who were so awful?'

'Her grandparents, of course.' Then Harriet clutched her chest and her colour faded. 'Ooh... I think it's starting again.'

'Let's get you through to Intensive Care,' Blake snapped, annoyed with himself for being diverted. He motioned to the nurse at the head of the trolley. 'Now.'

Blake refused point-blank to think about Nell for the rest of the evening. Not once. Or not once very much.

Harriet refused to be transferred to Blairglen. Well, why should she leave Sandy Ridge? She was sure Dr Blake would look after her beautifully, just as well as any of the clever doctors at Blairglen, and she thought she was paying Blake a compliment by staying put.

As did all the locals. They refused to take themselves to the major hospital, supremely confident that Dr Blake would look after them.

Dr Blake and whose army? he thought wearily for what must be the thousandth time since he'd taken over here.

But... 'We don't need another doctor,' he found himself telling Grace Mayne as he finally had a cup of tea with the old fisherwoman. Grace's husband had died just a couple of months ago and she was desperately lonely. Her only son had drowned when he'd been little more than a teenager, and now she had no one.

Blake had liked Grace at first sight. She was tough, wiry, belligerent, and as huge-hearted a woman as he'd ever met. The weeks since her husband's death had cast her into deep depression, so Blake had found himself dropping in frequently—just to see her. Tonight the last thing he wanted was to socialise, but he forced himself to pause, take a seat at the old lady's kitchen table and accept her hospitality.

The alternative might be worse, he thought. He'd watched Grace's face as they'd buried her husband, and he found himself increasingly concerned as to her welfare. There'd been one tragedy after another in the old lady's life. This last death had left her feeling desolate—so desolate that he wondered how she could keep going. He watched her take her fishing boat out through the heads, and each time he saw the little boat make the run he wondered whether she'd come back.

And if she didn't, he'd feel dreadful. So he made time to call and chat, even though a million other things were pressing. Tonight the most obvious thing to talk about was Nell. After all, the rest of the town was talking about her. Why not Blake?

And Grace was definitely interested. 'Nell McKenzie…' The woman's sea-bleached eyes narrowed. 'You mean the lass who was brought up here with Doc and Mrs McKenzie?'

'That's the one.'

'I remember when Nell left for university,' she said slowly. 'Haven't seen her since.'

'No one has. But it seems she wants to come back here to live.'

Grace thought it through and shook her head in disbelief. 'I don't know why. The town made life miserable for her.'

'Did it?' Blake was pleased. He'd caused a spark of interest, which was more than the old lady had shown for a long time.

'Yeah. Or her grandparents did and we didn't object.' Grace stared reflectively into her nearly empty teacup and, to Blake's astonishment, something akin to a smile played around her mouth. 'Nell McKenzie. Well, well.'

'Well, well.' Blake cast a curious glance across the table. 'You sound like you know her fairly well.'

'No. No one does. No one was allowed to know her.'

'Why not?'

But Grace wasn't answering. She was staring into the dregs of her tea like she was staring into the past, but the smile remained on her face.

At least she wasn't suicidal tonight, Blake thought thankfully, rising to leave. He'd given her something to think about, even though he didn't understand why she was so interested.

But at least she *was* interested, and for that Blake could only be thankful.

It was after midnight when Blake drove home from the last house call and it was all he could do to keep himself awake. He opened the car windows wide, he turned the radio up full blast, but he knew he was still in danger of going to sleep at the wheel.

Back at the hospital he checked on Harriet who was sleeping soundly, hooked up to the heart monitor. If he could keep her quiet she might well stay that way until morning.

It seemed there was a block of some kind, he thought as he examined the results of his tests. There was no evidence of heart-muscle injury on the cardiograph or in the blood tests, but she had a very slow pulse.

She needs a cardiologist, Blake thought, and maybe a pacemaker and he knew it'd take him hours the next morning to convince her that he couldn't fit her with a pacemaker on his own. She'd have to go to Blairglen.

Finally, almost asleep on his feet, he pushed open the door between the hospital and his living quarters. And he stopped dead.

Nell was waiting for him.

'You've been ages,' she told him. 'I knew you'd be late but this is ridiculous.'

'What?' He was so exhausted he was having trouble taking it all in.

First of all, Nell had been transformed. No longer in purple overalls, she was now dressed in a bright crimson, floor-length bathrobe. It had rich burgundy lining, it was big enough to wrap around her twice, and she was curled up on the sofa with her bare toes poking out, looking like…

Looking like he didn't know what.

And what on earth was she sitting on? Where was his horrible settee? Where was his dining setting?

The sofa Nell was sitting on was enormous. It was ancient, a great mass of soft velvet cushions. Like her amazing dressing-gown, it was vivid crimson. It was the sort of sofa you just wanted to sink in and...

And nothing!

'What have you done to my house?' he managed, and if his voice came out strangled who could blame him?

'It's *our* house,' she reminded him gently. 'As an employed doctor in the town I have just as many rights to this place as you do. Don't you like it?' She gazed up at him, a picture of injured innocence. 'I've gone to so much trouble. And do you like my dressing-gown?' She beamed down at her splendid self. 'This belonged to Grandpa. Such a waste.'

'But—'

'I've been so busy...'

'I can see that.' He was still taking everything in. What was new?

Everything was new.

The vinyl furniture had disappeared completely. There was now the amazing sofa and a couple of great squishy armchairs. There was a new dining table—or rather an old one—an oak affair that looked as if it had been polished for generations. There were matching dining chairs with scatter cushions. And rugs...three vast Turkish rugs covering almost every available piece of floor space.

There were even pictures on the walls!

'Did this all come out of your suitcase?' he enquired, and she chuckled.

'I just waved my magic wand.'

He glanced at his watch. He'd been away for exactly five hours.

'You just nipped out to the shops, then. Or called in a decorator?'

'Well, no.'

'So would you like to explain?'

'I went exploring and caught Bob and Henry before they left the hospital.'

He thought that one through. Bob and Henry. He only knew the one Bob and Henry pair. 'The ambulance drivers?'

'I know them both from way back,' she told him. 'They weren't ambulance drivers in my day. In fact, I went to school with Bob, and when I showed him the conditions we were expected to live in he was shocked. Both of them were.'

'He's given you this stuff?' Blake's voice was unbelieving, and Nell giggled.

'No, silly. It's from my house.'

'Your house.'

'I told you,' she said patiently. 'I own a house out on the bluff. It's ancient, it hasn't been used for years but it's full of extremely good stuff. Like this.' She patted her sofa fondly. 'I knew it'd be comfortable. I was never allowed to sit on it when I was a kid but, oh, how I wanted to.'

He was distracted—almost—but there were burning questions. 'How the hell did you get this stuff back here?'

'The ambulance, of course,' she said blithely. 'How else?'

'You used the ambulance to transport furniture?' He was gearing himself up to explode.

'If I hadn't then I'd have needed the ambulance tomorrow to cart me away for major back repair.' Her tone was innocence personified. 'It was a case of preventative medicine, and I'm really good at that. I was determined to get it here, and my little sedan only has a very tiny roof-rack. Anyway, once I explained the situation to Henry and Bob they were only too pleased to help.' She smiled up at Blake. 'So we took the stretchers out of the ambulance and went for it. It took us five trips and we've only just finished.'

'And if there'd been an urgent call?'

'Then they'd have heaved the furniture out and got on

with it,' she told him. 'Honestly—do you think we're negligent or something?'

He thought no such thing. He didn't know what to think. He walked over and sank down into one of the chairs—and promptly stood up again.

One of the cushions had moved! Now it rose, shoving itself to four feet, and it glared at him. What the...?

But Nell was smiling. 'Um...meet Ernest. Dr Sutherland, Ernest. Ernest, meet Dr Sutherland.'

'Ernest.'

Who was Ernest? He'd just found out. Blake found himself looking at the most mournful, pathetic bag of bones he'd ever come across in the doggy kingdom. The ancient cocker spaniel, his black and white coat faded with age into indiscriminate grey, was all jowls and floppy ears and huge mournful eyes. He looked up at Blake as if he'd just wounded him to the core.

'Hey, I didn't sit on you,' Blake said before he could help himself. 'I nearly did but I didn't.'

The eyes still reproached him.

'Oh, for heaven's sake...'

'Take no notice of him,' Nell said blithely. 'Ernest's greatest skill in life is making people feel guilty, whether they deserve it or not.'

'He does a great job.'

'He does.' Nell grinned. 'I adopted him because he looked so pathetic. It's his principal talent and he's really very good.' She rose and crossed to give her dog a hug. 'I've had him for five months now. It's been a guilt trip all the way, yet still I love him.'

Blake was still taking things on board. 'This is the Ernest that's going to take up the third bedroom?'

'Well, I'm not going to sleep with him,' Nell said, horrified. 'He snores.'

Blake looked down at the ancient Ernest and he grinned.

'He looks like the sort of dog who'd snore.'

He got a really, really reproachful canine glare for his pains.

'Ernest's very sensitive,' Nell warned. 'You might find you have to pay for that remark.'

'He doesn't bite?'

'Bite?' Nell shook her head in disbelief. She crossed to the little kitchenette and opened the oven door. 'That requires energy. No, Ernest's principal way of punishing people is by ignoring them.'

'I can live with that.'

'You'll find you can't,' she warned him. 'It's very effective. He sort of embellishes his ignoring routine in all sorts of fancy ways. You'll see. Now… Dinner?'

Ernest was promptly forgotten. 'Dinner!'

'You haven't eaten?' She turned back to face him. 'I didn't see how you could have.'

'No, but—'

'Then there's dinner,' she told him as if he were stupid. 'I ate hours ago but I saved half the casserole for you. It's apricot chicken. Very basic but it is my first night. We stopped off at the all-nighter on our first furniture run so I could throw this together while the boys heaved sofas.' And then she grinned. 'I imagine it's set the town talking. An ambulance parked outside the minimart with a sofa sticking out the back.'

He imagined it might have. He should be angry. But there was apricot chicken casserole. His nose was giving him all sorts of messages, and every one of them was urgent.

And it was sort of funny…

'I don't approve,' he managed, and Nell nodded.

'Of course you don't. You're a very responsible doctor. I can see that. So you don't approve of ambulances filled with sofas, buying chicken drumsticks and cans of apricots. But you will still eat my casserole?'

He was trying hard not to laugh. For heaven's sake, she was ridiculous. 'I might.'

'Ernest will if you don't,' she said cheerfully, and Blake turned and glowered at the dog. Ernest glowered back.

But this was a dog after all. 'Don't even think about it,' Blake told him. 'Not even the scraps.'

'He's already eaten,' Nell said.

'Chicken casserole?'

'Dog food. The ambulance and sofa brought that, too. But he's not fussy and he's always up for second helpings.'

'I imagine he might be. That's quite some paunch.'

'Now you really are getting personal.' She scooped the casserole onto a plate and set it down on her gorgeous table. The whole room came together. The aroma of the delicious casserole. The furniture. The dog. The brilliantly dressed woman, heavily pregnant, ladling out food…

It was the sort of scenario that'd normally make him run a mile.

'Wrap yourself around that,' Nell told him, and she smiled.

Who could resist an invitation like that?

'Wash your dishes afterwards,' she said blithely. She hauled her dog up into her arms. 'We've done enough. Ernest and I are very, very tired and we're off to bed. We'll leave you to it.'

She left, and the room was desolate for her going.

CHAPTER THREE

SOMEONE was trying to smother him.

Blake woke to fur balls. Or fur mats. Something warm and heavy and limp was lying right across his face, threatening to choke him while he slept. He sat up like he'd been shot, and Ernest slid sideways onto the floor.

The stupid dog lay like he was paralysed, four legs in the air, eyes frantic, waiting for someone to set him to rights. Good grief!

'You dopey dog. Don't you have any respect?'

Ernest whimpered.

Was the creature injured? Blake flung back the covers, climbed out of bed and stooped to see.

Ernest promptly found his feet, took one agile leap and landed in the warm spot vacated by Blake.

'You damned dog… You're out of here.' Blake put a hand on his collar to haul him away, but it was easier said than done. Ernest lay like a dead dog. His eyes were closed and he snoozed as if he'd been asleep for hours, seemingly totally oblivious of anyone else's comfort but his own.

'It's either you or me, mate,' Blake muttered, and glanced at the clock. And then glanced again. Hell. That couldn't be right. The clock said eight-thirty. His alarm was set for six.

The alarm had been turned off.

She'd sneaked in while he'd been sleeping, he thought incredulously, and then wondered how on earth could she have done it. He would have woken. Surely?

The thought of Nell tiptoeing across his bedroom had him as unnerved as…as did her stupid dog sleeping in his bed!

'OK. I know. I have to get up,' he told Ernest. 'Sure, you can use my bed. Any time. Don't mind me.'

Ernest didn't.

He'd have to skip breakfast. There was a ward round to do before surgery at nine, and there wasn't time. At least no one had rung during the night, he thought as he showered and dressed, but that in itself was unusual. Worrying even.

He'd had the best sleep he'd had in months and he felt like a million dollars for it, but he'd have to pay by working doubly hard now. Harriet's heart problems needed urgent attention. He needed to persuade her to be transferred at least to Blairglen but preferably to one of the major coronary-care units at Sydney or Melbourne. That by itself would take hours.

Damn, damn, damn…

And on the other side of the wall, Nell must still be in bed.

'She's been a great help,' he told Ernest as he hauled a comb through his unruly thatch of hair. 'Some Christmas present she turns out to be. She turns off my alarm, she lands me with her dog and then she sleeps in…'

She was seven months pregnant. And she *had* made him apricot chicken the night before.

'But I don't need domesticity,' he told the somnolent Ernest. 'I'd rather eat baked beans on toast and be on time. How on earth can I fit everything in?' He slammed the bedroom door on the sleeping dog, walked out through the living room—trying to ignore just how good the newly furnished room looked in the early morning light—and stalked through to the hospital.

'Some Christmas present,' he muttered again, anger building at the thought of what lay ahead. 'Now I'll be late all day.'

Only he wasn't. Everything had been done.

Donald, the charge nurse, came to greet him, his face

wreathed in smiles. 'Well, well, if it's not Captain Snooze. Our Dr McKenzie told us you were having a wee sleep in and we could hardly believe it.'

'*Your* Dr McKenzie?'

'She's been here for two hours,' Donald told him. 'She had breakfast with the staff and we feel we've really got to know her. She's a great kid.' Donald was fifty. Anyone forty-nine or under was a kid to him—Blake included. Now he beamed like a Scottish patriarch, solving the problems of the world.

'And she's very, very competent,' Donald told him, ignoring the look on Blake's face and sounding as pleased as Punch. 'Louise couldn't get Elmer Jefferson's drip back in last night and she did it first go. Louise says she has fingers like you wouldn't believe.'

'You've let her near the patients?' Blake's voice rose to incredulous and Donald took a step back—but he wasn't a nurse to be intimidated by a mere doctor. They worked on equal footing, these two.

'Now, why wouldn't I have done that?' he demanded. 'Don't be a fool, man. She's a registered doctor, she's approved and paid by our hospital board, and Jonas and Emily from Bay Beach both rang me up personally to vouch for her training. I knew her when she was a kid, so I was tickled pink to hear she was coming back.'

Tickled pink hardly described how *he* was feeling. Blake stared at his charge nurse through narrowed eyes. 'You *knew* she was coming?'

'We all did,' Donald said smugly. 'Happy Christmas, Dr Sutherland.'

Great. The world had gone mad.

'Where is she now?'

'She's done a full ward round, sorted out any problems— not that there were any—only Elmer at five a.m.'

'Elmer's drip packed up at five and you didn't ring me? You know he—'

'Yeah, we know it's important. That septicaemia isn't

going to go away without a few more days of antibiotics. It was some spider bite he got.' He grinned, enjoying Blake's annoyance. 'So Louise rang Nell—just like she told us to.'

'When did she tell you to?'

'Last night, of course.' Donald grinned again. 'A couple of the nurses stopped by to lend her a hand with the furniture moving when they finished late shift. Me included. She got us hanging pictures and said you were taking turns with calls, starting last night, so when the drip packed up at five Louise rang her.'

'Rang my phone? I would have heard.'

'Louise rang Nell's cellphone,' Donald said patiently. 'She gave us the number. Easy.'

Easy...

His life had been turned upside down. By a nutcase.

'Is she wearing her purple patchwork pants?' he couldn't help asking, and this time it was Donald's turn to look astonished.

'Now, why should she wear purple patchwork to work? She's a professional. No. She's wearing a white coat over some sort of floral skirt. Very demure. See for yourself. She's in with Harriet.'

'Harriet?'

'Harriet's been busy planning how you could perform open-heart surgery here,' Donald told him, grinning. 'She wouldn't take no for an answer. I told Nell what the problem was and Nell left her until last. So she's still there. Want to see how she's doing?'

Blake did. He cast one more glare at his charge nurse—heck, Donald almost sounded as if he'd been bewitched—and then he stalked off down the corridor to Intensive Care. To see what damage had been done, and how best he could undo it.

Only, of course, no damage had been done at all. Harriet was lying back on her pillows, smiling up at the woman beside her bed, and Nell was holding her hand.

The night and the chest pain had taken their toll on Harriet. Her bravado of the night before had slipped, and fear was showing through. She was gripping Nell's hand like she was drawing strength from human contact.

She looked up as Blake entered—they both did—and he received two smiles of welcome. Nell's was warm and open. Harriet's was a bit wobbly.

'Dr Sutherland…'

He had the sense to focus on Harriet first. Nell and her damned managerial ways could wait.

'Hey there.' He walked across, took the old lady's hand away from Nell and held it himself. 'Well done,' he told her. 'You've had the night without any more trouble.' And then he frowned and looked sideways at Nell. 'At least, I assume there was no more trouble.'

'I would have woken you if there was,' Nell said blithely, and he almost choked.

Focus on Harriet…

'No more palpitations?'

'Nothing.'

'Great.' He hesitated. 'Harriet, we're going to have to get specialist opinion on this. I'm afraid that means a trip…'

'To Sydney.' Harriet managed a brave smile. 'I know. Nell…Dr McKenzie's just been explaining it to me.'

'Call me Nell,' Nell said promptly. 'Please. You used to call me Nell when I was a little girl. I don't see why you should change now.' She smiled fondly down at the old lady. 'Harriet used to run the general store and sometimes she gave me free sweets,' she explained to Blake, and Harriet's smile died.

'It was the least I could do. No one else ever did. Those dreadful—'

'That's enough,' Nell told her. 'The bad old days are over. Forgotten. And now aren't I lucky? Being a doctor, I can buy all the sweets I want.'

'Oh, my dear…'

But Nell was refusing sympathy. 'I've just been telling Harriet about my friend Matt who's the head of Coronary Care at Sydney Central.' She turned to Blake. 'Matt's a real sweetheart. He has a gorgeous wife and he has two sets of twins and a dog just like Ernest. In fact, he's Ernest's brother.'

Despite himself, Blake grinned at that one. 'Matt's Ernest's brother?' he asked incredulously. 'Don't go near him with a bargepole, Harriet. Ernest is the dopiest—'

'Matt's *dog* is Ernest's brother,' Nell said with dignity, but her green eyes twinkled. 'And haven't you made it up with my dog yet?'

'Two dogs like Ernest...' Blake said, raising his eyes to the ceiling, and Nell's twinkle deepened.

'Yep. Aren't they just wonderful?'

'Wonderful!'

Nell gazed at him thoughtfully for a long moment—and then shook her head. She put her mind back to business. 'Anyway, Harriet thinks she might just trust Matt to decide what's best to be done, so I've organised an air transfer to Sydney.'

'You've organised an air transfer?'

'With Donald's help, of course,' she told him. 'We decided Bob and Henry weren't really skilled enough for a coronary-care transfer.'

'And if Bob spends the day with the ambulance it'd mean the mail would be really late—if it arrived at all—and it's so near Christmas that it'd be a disaster,' Harriet chirped in, and Blake could only stare.

'But...'

'But what, Dr Sutherland?' Nell smiled. 'We haven't set in motion anything that you can't rescind. The air ambulance doesn't arrive until midday. But Harriet and I agree that you have quite enough on your plate without trying to implant a pacemaker before Christmas.'

'Harriet's agreed to this?'

'If Matt thinks it's necessary. Harriet wants to hang

around for the long term. She's agreed to help me set my house in order—oh, and knit me one of her famous capes. She knitted one for my grandmother once and I did so want one.'

'If I'd known,' Harriet said darkly, and Nell shook her head.

'No. How could you know? But now you do and you've agreed to make it for me so I'll have the wool ready as soon as you're transferred back. And I'll also ring Sonia, Matt's wife. She'll bring her latest set of twins in to see you and I'll bet she has you knitting for them before you can blink.'

Nell was fantastic, Blake thought reluctantly. Absolutely fantastic. In one fell swoop she'd persuaded Harriet to go to Sydney, she'd organised her company while she was there, she'd taken the depersonalisation out of Harriet's medical process—when Harriet met Matt she wouldn't think of him as a cardiologist but as the father of two sets of twins and one dopey dog—and Nell had given her something to look forward to on her return.

Whew!

'I probably need to go now,' Nell told Harriet, smiling down at her like a co-conspirator. 'I'm just about ready for a cup of coffee, and I'll bet Dr Sutherland wants to examine you.'

'There's probably no need,' Harriet said, but her eyes twinkled up at Nell. 'Oh, very well. We don't want to put his nose out of joint, I suppose.'

'Of course we don't.' Nell stooped and kissed her. '*That* would be perfectly appalling.'

He found Nell fifteen minutes later. She was sitting in the hospital kitchen, tucking into an enormous plate of eggs and bacon. As soon as he arrived she waved to the stove.

'Yours is there. Cook made it for you. I told her you were coming. If you're quick the eggs will still be runny.'

'I don't have time to eat.'

'Of course you have time to eat,' she said firmly. 'It's one of life's imperatives. Mrs Condie will be back in a few minutes and if she finds you haven't eaten it she'll be very hurt—especially when I told her how hungry you were.'

Was there no end to this woman's interference? 'How did you know I was hungry? I could have had breakfast at home.'

'I saw what was in your refrigerator,' she said darkly. 'Green bread, and bacon to match. Even Ernest would turn up his nose at that.'

The smell was delicious. She was infuriating—but she was also right. OK, he'd eat. To refuse would be petty. 'Ernest eats fillet steak, does he?' he muttered, scooping bacon and eggs onto a plate.

'If he can get it. Why wouldn't he?'

'Why indeed?'

Her green eyes widened. 'You don't like my dog?'

'Your dog,' he said with a glower, hunkering down in a chair on the other side of the table, 'is currently sleeping in my bed. *My bed!*'

'Whoops,' she said contritely. 'I couldn't have pulled the door fully shut when I switched off your alarm.'

'Now, about that—'

'Eat your breakfast before it gets cold,' she told him, popping another bacon rasher between her teeth. 'This is yummy.'

Blake ate a bacon rasher. And then another. And he glowered all the time.

'The wind'll change,' she said kindly.

'Excuse me?'

'If you keep that horrid expression on your face you could be in real trouble. I'm sure you don't mean to look bad-tempered, but if the wind changes while you look that way then you're stuck with it for life.'

'That's superstitious nonsense.'

'Oh, no. My best friend told me that when I was five so I'm sure it must be right.'

'Dr McKenzie—'

'Nell.'

'Dr McKenzie,' he repeated through clenched teeth.

'I suppose it's better than Miss McKenzie.' She sighed. 'What?'

'You had no business turning off my alarm clock.'

'But you were tired and I'm your Christmas present.' She said it as if it made everything fine.

'You still had no business interfering, and as for taking *my* calls in the night…'

'That's what I'm here for—and they're not *your* calls. They're *our* calls. The hospital board's employing me, so you have no right to act as if everything medical is yours. Now, this morning—'

'You've done enough already. This morning you can take yourself off.'

'Nope. I've organised it all with Marion.'

'You've what?'

'Organised with our receptionist,' she told him sweetly. 'She's pulled out all the patient files and I thought I'd run through them with you now. Before I see patients.'

'But *I'll* be seeing patients.'

'*You'll* see patients this afternoon.' She smiled again. 'I expect I'll be feeling a bit weary by this afternoon so I imagine I might take an afternoon nap, so you can take over all you want. Then.'

'Dr—'

'Won't you call me Nell?'

'It's impossible,' he burst out, and slammed his fist down on the table. Her coffee-cup jumped and coffee sloshed into the saucer. He glared across the table and found she was surveying him with care.

'You have a temper,' she said.

'*I* have a temper?' He thought back to the day before. 'How about you?'

She considered that, and found it reasonable. 'OK, we both have tempers, so let's moderate. Marion says you have any number of house calls banked up. The district nurse has a list and she says you've been going through them on a priority basis. But she says a morning off surgery would let you get the worst of them cleared. Is that right?'

Blake thought it through. 'Yes, I suppose so.'

'So there you go. I would appreciate it if you could run through the patient list with me first. Just so I know who's a hypochondriac and who's likely to be in trouble.' She smiled. 'I do miss the good old days before lawsuits where you could write ''complete and utter nutcase'' in the patient's history and get away with it.'

He struggled against a smile. 'But…'

'But what? Is that all you ever say?' Suddenly exasperated, Nell laid down her knife and fork and pushed back her plate. 'Are you still intent on arguing? Dr Sutherland, what have you got against me seeing our patients while you do our house calls?'

Our.

The word took Blake aback. It was a word that hadn't entered his vocabulary for two years. *Our…*

'I guess—'

'It's sensible,' she said firmly. 'Isn't it?'

It was. It was also…wonderful. To clean up his outstanding house calls… Whew!

'Now, you don't have to do them all today,' Nell urged, seeing where his thoughts were headed. 'I'll be here again tomorrow so you don't need to clear the decks completely. Marion thought you could spend a couple of hours doing home visits, then come back and take a run on the beach before lunch.'

'What business is it of—?'

But Nell was unstoppable. She had it all figured out. 'Marion says that's your very favourite thing and you haven't been able to go for a proper run for months. You've had to run near the hospital so you're available for emergencies. But today you can run where you want. Then you can come back about one o'clock, shower, lunch and be bright-eyed and bushy-tailed for afternoon surgery.'

'You have it all organised.'

'That's what I'm here for.' She rose and took her dishes to the sink. 'And you can't fight city hall. So you'd best just roll with the punches, Dr Sutherland. And who knows? You might even end up enjoying it.'

How could he enjoy it?

Blake spent the morning doing house calls but his thoughts flew back to the surgery at every available minute. What was Nell doing? Who was she seeing?

'I hear we've got a new lady doctor,' old Desmond Scott told him as he dressed his ulcerated legs, and Blake couldn't keep back the grimace.

'Is she that bad?' Des asked sympathetically.

Blake caught himself at that. What had Daniel at Sydney Central told him? *She's extremely competent...* Coming from Daniel, that was praise indeed.

So what on earth was he worrying about? he demanded of himself. Why couldn't he simply roll with the punches and enjoy it?

Because Nell was...bossy?

'Women make a real difference around the place,' Desmond ventured, seeing his thoughts stray sideways and trying to guess the reason. 'They stick their noses into everything. Can't help themselves. And they say she's moved into your house. You'll have a filing cabinet in the bathroom with a drawer marked ''Razor'' before you know it. And you'll be in trouble for leaving the toilet seat up! You mark my words.'

'There speaks a long-married man.' Blake relaxed a bit and allowed himself to grin. OK, maybe he was overreacting slightly.

'My Lorna would organise from dawn to dusk and never be happier,' Desmond told him proudly. 'She's gone across to her sister's now with a casserole because Madge is poorly, and she'll be so mad that you've come while she's away. She likes being here when you come, so she can give you a cup of tea and have a bit of gossip on the side. House calls in surgery hours is not what we're used to.' He chortled. 'I guess she'll have to get used to them now, though. This new doctor will free you up to do your house calls whenever. That'll mess with Lorna's routine no end.'

'Dr McKenzie's only here for four weeks.'

Des frowned at that. 'That's not what I hear. Grace Mayne popped in earlier this morning and she reckons she's home for good.'

'She's having a baby.'

'So Grace said, but should that stop her working? There's plenty of women these days work with a littly.'

Blake carefully re-dressed the worst of the ulcers, concentrating on the wounds rather than allowing himself to think about Nell being here permanently. Desmond's ulcers were deep and nasty. The old man's skin was like fine parchment stretched taut across the bone, and the least scratch turned into a mess. Usually dressing his ulcers upset him so it was good to see his attention diverted, even if it was toward the new lady doctor.

'We'll see,' Blake told him. 'There's time enough to worry about how much she works after she has the baby. And she can't stay in Sandy Ridge to have it.'

'You won't deliver her?'

'You know as well as I do that I need back-up if I'm to set myself up for deliveries.' Des was the retired town pharmacist and enjoyed talking medicine. In the interminable time it was taking to treat Desmond's succession of ulcers, they often talked about the problems of Blake's practice.

'I guess you have antenatal back-up now,' Des said thoughtfully. 'With Nell here you can deliver anyone but her.'

Blake applied the last of the adhesive and stood up, thinking it through. Des was right. Maybe he wouldn't make a habit of delivering babies—he'd still like a paediatrician on call before he did that—but he was better able to cope with emergencies now. Not just for antenatal work. For everything.

It was a really strange feeling. There was someone right at this minute doing the work he usually did, and the thought was taking some time to sink in.

He had back-up. Up until now he'd been too wearily confused and hostile to see it. Now he drove home and let himself think about what that back-up could mean.

The possibilities were endless.

He thought of Lyn Slater. Lyn was due to deliver in two weeks and the rule was to leave town and find somewhere to stay in Blairglen at least two weeks before the baby was due. But Lyn had been holding out until the last minute. She had two other children and hated the thought of uprooting the family for Christmas.

The risks of delivering her had been a burden on his tired mind. Now at least they could cope with a Caesarean if they had to.

So Nell's Christmas present would be a gift not just to him. Nell could help him improve the standard of care to the whole district. If she was competent.

She's extremely competent, Daniel had said.

The thought was suddenly immeasurably exciting.

If only she wasn't so damned infuriating. So damned bossy. But what else had Daniel said?

She's such a mousy little thing.

If only she was, Blake thought grimly. Sure, it'd be great having a competent doctor around for Christmas, but she wouldn't be much help if she was strangled before Christmas Eve.

She'd told him to run. He did six house calls and was tempted to do more, but Nell's words rang in his ears. Go for a run on the beach… He hadn't run on the beach for months!

His running was his time-out. His only time-out. Ever since Sylvia… Well, ever since he'd needed to, he'd escaped into himself by running. He'd pound the pavements until his heart thumped inside his chest and the pain around his heart eased because there simply wasn't room for pain and exhaustion at the same time. Running had become almost a drug. He'd run or he'd go nuts, so every day, no matter how exhausted he was, he'd don running gear and do some miles.

And the beach here was lovely—long and golden and sun-drenched, it stretched for miles. The thought of it now was almost irresistible.

He shouldn't do it. He should go back to the surgery. But finally he couldn't withstand Nell's offer. He headed back to the house, disturbed Ernest's steady snooze, enquired politely if Ernest would like a run, too—well, you had to be courteous about these things, but Ernest looked at him like he'd lost his mind—and then headed to the beach.

He ran for an hour. Half an hour north. Half an hour south. Then, on impulse, because it was a gorgeous day and he may as well go for broke, he ran into the water and swam like a ten-year-old.

When he turned to the shore there was a woman and a dog sitting on the beach, watching. Nell and Ernest.

CHAPTER FOUR

HE WAS quite something, Nell thought dispassionately as she watched Blake come out of the water. If she was interested in men—which she wasn't—and if she was into bodies that looked like they'd come out of the centrefolds of *Women Only*, then maybe…

But she definitely wasn't. No.

'I've been stupid enough in that direction to last a lifetime,' she told Ernest, hugging him close. 'You're the only man in my life from now on.'

But there was no harm in watching.

Blake had hauled off his shirt and running shoes before he'd entered the water and he'd swum in his shorts. 'That's quite a six-pack,' Nell told Ernest knowledgeably, looking at the muscles rippling across Blake's chest and abdomen. 'Wow!' Then she looked down at Ernest's saggy midriff and grinned. 'Something you can only dream about.'

Ernest looked up and licked her.

'You don't want a body to die for?' Nell's grin widened and she hugged him again. 'I don't think Blake does either,' she told her dog. 'Em says he lost his wife three years ago and has been driven ever since. That's why he runs. It's also why he's not sure he wants me here.'

She thought back to the conversation she'd had with her friend when they'd been arranging this deal.

'He doesn't stop for a minute,' Em had told her. 'Maybe if he really tried he could get a partner at Sandy Ridge— or maybe Chris would have stayed on and worked part time in semi-retirement. But no. Blake has to take the weight of the world on his shoulders, and if he's not frantic with medicine he runs as if the world's chasing him. It's like if he stops the pain's going to catch up.'

'Was his wife really special?' Nell had enquired, and Em had shaken her head.

'I don't think she was, and I think that's the cause of the trouble.'

'I don't understand.'

'It's not my business to explain,' Em had said primly. Then she'd looked at Nell and her primness had faded to mischief. 'At least, that's what Jonas tells me, and I'm sure it means he doesn't know either. We're only going on hints of medical gossip and they lived in Western Australia before she died, which means the gossip's not very forthcoming. So you'll just have to find out for yourself!'

Drat! But there was enough to go on that was intriguing. Nell sighed. Then she went back to watching Blake walk out of the shallows, admiring the splendid muscles of the man—and waiting for him to register that she was sitting on the beach.

He couldn't get away from her. It was weird, coming out of the water and finding her there. It felt like a huge intrusion into his personal space.

People didn't wait for Blake Sutherland. Not like this.

But Nell was definitely waiting. She was wearing a maternity dress today. It wasn't as loud as her patchwork overalls. It was pretty and flowing—he'd glimpsed it under her white coat this morning—but now, on the beach, it was summery and nice and...

For heaven's sake, what was he doing, noticing what she was wearing? he demanded of himself. What did it matter? And she'd brought her blasted dog to the beach. Why? It wasn't as if Ernest was the slightest bit interested in exercise.

He glanced at his watch, suddenly hopeful. Afternoon surgery was due to start at two. Maybe he was rushed.

Damn. It wasn't yet one. He wasn't rushed at all and the novelty of being unrushed was almost indescribable.

But he still felt trapped. He saw her watching him—waiting—and there was nothing to do but to towel himself dry and stroll on up the beach, as if meeting pregnant women and crazy dogs on gorgeously sunlit beaches was something he did every day of his life.

'I've brought sandwiches.' She didn't greet him as such—just motioned to her picnic basket, and by the look of the crammed contents it didn't just hold sandwiches. It held a feast.

'You made this lot in between patients this morning?' he said in disbelief, and she chuckled.

'Yep. Superwoman. That's me.' Then she relented. 'Actually, Mrs Condie packed it up for me.'

The hospital cook. He frowned. At last—something he could object to. 'Mrs Condie has better things to be doing than making us picnics.'

'Hey, she offered,' Nell broke in before he could get any further. 'The staff were really pleased you'd found time for a run. I finished surgery, came out and discovered every nurse in the hospital knew you were down at the beach.' She grinned. 'Keeping secrets isn't this town's strong point. Anyway, I found this waiting for me on Marion's desk, with the suggestion that I might like lunch on the beach as well.' She beamed up at him. 'You know, you have very nice staff.'

He had very interfering staff.

'I need to go back.'

'To shower and change before afternoon surgery?' She nodded but she was flipping the cloth from the top of the basket. 'Sure, but you've got ages and there's chicken and avocado sandwiches. My favourite. And chocolate éclairs.'

He was backed up against a wall. 'I usually just have fruit for lunch.' It sounded pathetic, even to him.

'Then that's why you're skinny and I'm fat,' she said, and he grinned despite himself.

'No, Dr McKenzie. You're fat and I'm skinny because you're pregnant and I'm not pregnant. It has nothing to do with chocolate éclairs.'

Her twinkly eyes assessed him, running over the long lines of his body. She was assessing him the same way she'd have assessed a laboratory specimen, and he found the experience disconcerting to say the least. 'I guess you're not really skinny, but there's not an inch of spare fat on you,' she decided out loud. 'Whew. That's what the glossies call a body to die for.'

'What glossies?'

'Any glossies. Especially those ones that have six-pack men in the middle.'

'I'm amazed you read them.'

'They sure beat medical journals.' She grinned. 'Besides, I have high literary tastes,' she said with dignity. 'A girl has to keep informed of what's up to date. And in fashion.' Her eyes narrowed against the sun. 'I have to inform you— in case you don't already know—that your type of body is very much in fashion.'

'Gee, thanks.' He was so disconcerted he was almost at the blushing stage.

'Well, it's very nice,' she told him kindly. And then she sighed. 'I can tell you don't indulge in cream cakes too often. There's not a lot of chocolate éclairs in your biceps. I won't be as lean as you even after Brunhilda's born.'

That startled him out of his self-consciousness of standing semi-naked and discussing his body build... He clutched this new straw and held on.

'Brunhilda?'

'This baby's been kicking me all morning,' Nell told him. 'So I said one more kick and she was being christened Brunhilda. Or Cornelius if he's a boy.'

He grinned at that. She really was the most extraordinary woman. 'And he—or she—stopped kicking immediately?'

'Nope,' she said sadly, handing him up a sandwich. 'I can see I'm about to have discipline problems. Cornelius or Brunhilda kept right on kicking. So that's it. They're doomed till they can come of age and change their names by deed poll. Never make a threat you don't intend to keep, that was my grandma's motto, and that's what I intend…'

And then her voice faded a bit, as if memory was intruding. 'Well, never mind. Maybe I don't intend all that much. Go on. Wrap yourself around your sandwich. There's heaps more where they came from.'

Why had she suddenly gone quiet?

She had him intrigued, he realised. He sat on his towel and ate his sandwich—and then another—and then another after that because really they were extraordinarily good, and he realised he knew not the first thing about Nell. And something about the way she was looking now said that it might well be hard to find out.

'You were raised by your grandparents?' he asked, and her face shuttered.

'Yes.'

It was about as communicative as a closed door. He tried again.

'But there wasn't a lot of love lost between you?'

'You might say that. Hey, there's lamingtons in here. Well done, Mrs Condie. Yum.'

He refused to be diverted. 'What happened to your parents?'

'I don't know. Or at least I don't know much.'

That raised his eyebrows. 'What do you mean?'

'I mean I don't know who my father was, and my mother dumped me here with her parents when I was three months old and was never seen again.' She bit into her lamington reflectively. 'Not that I blame her for never coming back, mind you. My grandparents told me she wasn't married— a whore was how they described her. Intolerance personified, that was Grandmother and Grandfather. So Sandy

Ridge was hardly a great place in which to be a single mum.'

Blake eyed her speculatively. 'And yet you've returned—presumably to bring up your baby alone.'

'My grandparents are dead,' she told him as if that explained all. 'There's the difference. I dare say if my grandparents were alive you'd have had second thoughts about living here, too.'

'As bad as that?'

'Worse.'

'Want to talk about it?'

'Nope.'

'Why not?

Attack was the best form of defence. 'Want to tell me about your marriage?'

'Um…no.'

'There you go, then.' Subject closed. 'Ernest, I believe this sandwich is spare. Can I interest you—?'

She got no further. She definitely could interest Ernest. He was very much a sandwich-eating dog. Or an éclair-eating dog. Or lamington. Or whatever…

Their picnic finished, the last scraps enjoyed to the full by garbage-bin Ernest, they were left with silence. Somewhat to Blake's surprise it wasn't an uncomfortable silence. They sat on and watched the sea, and their thoughts went in all sorts of directions, but it was an easy peace now that was settling between them.

Truce…

He had a partner, Blake thought, and the enormity of what was being offered slammed home once again. Someone to share his workload. Someone to give him time to run…

'You know, you don't always have to run,' she said into the silence, and it was as if she'd read his thoughts. His eyes widened but she ignored his surprise to continue. 'Beaches are good for lying on, too. Trust me. I know this. Sleeping in the sun is one of my splinter skills.'

He thought about it. Sleeping in the sun... Why would he do that? 'I enjoy running,' he said brusquely.

She nodded. 'I'm sure you do—like we both enjoy medicine. But there's more to life than medicine and running.'

'Such as?'

'Such as looking at glossy centrefolds. Or decorating a Christmas tree,' she told him, suddenly sounding annoyed. 'Which brings me to my next point. I can't believe you haven't done it. So tonight, after surgery, is decreed a Christmas-tree-decorating session. Write it in your diary in black ink. "Eight p.m. Help Nell with tree." Got it?'

'I'll be busy.'

'You'll be busy decorating the tree.'

'Nell...'

'Hey, you didn't call me Dr McKenzie.' She beamed. 'There's an improvement.'

He corrected himself. 'Dr—'

'You're slipping. It's Nell.'

'I might be very grateful for your offer to share my workload,' he said stiffly. 'But that doesn't mean I'm welcoming you to share my life.'

For heaven's sake—she was only asking him to decorate a tree. He was overreacting here, and the lurking twinkle behind her eyes told him she knew it.

'Now, whatever made you think I wanted to do that?' she asked, incredulous. 'I've done that once before, thank you very much. Shared my life with a man. And if you think I'm going down that road again, you're very much mistaken.'

'I didn't mean sharing in that way.'

'I know you didn't,' she approved. 'If you had, I'd be out of here. But decorating a Christmas tree's not sharing a life. It's just a part of sharing a house. Sharing a Christmas. They're very different things, Dr Sutherland.'

He could only agree. But he looked at the way she was looking at him, and he wasn't so sure.

She was a mind-reader, and the thought was very, very threatening.

Afternoon surgery was endless, if only because every single patient wanted to know about Nell. They remembered her from years back and were amazed.

'Is it true Nell McKenzie's back in town? And now she's a doctor like her grandpa was? Well, who'd have thought it? She was such a quiet little thing. And she's pregnant, they say? Poor lamb, just like her mother. Well, at least she doesn't have to face that harridan of a grandmother.'

Blake listened politely and fielded the questions as best he could, but over and over he found himself aching to ask questions himself. Somehow he forced himself not to, because if he asked questions about Nell, he decided, then it was possible she could ask questions of him, and he didn't want to think where that could lead.

They weren't sharing a life. They were sharing a house—and Christmas—and even that seemed threatening.

Finally he finished. He saw his last patient at about six, and then spent some time flicking through the histories of the patients Nell had seen that morning. He found her notes meticulous and she'd made no decision he wouldn't have made himself.

So, yes, she was competent, but somehow it didn't make him feel any better about what was happening. Sure, his workload had eased, but in its place was a problem. Invasion of personal space... He didn't like it. He didn't want it and he hadn't asked for it.

Eight o'clock came all too soon. Christmas-tree-decorating time. Write it in your diary in black ink, she'd ordered, but he hadn't needed to. It was indelibly planted in his mind. How could he avoid it?

But then... They couldn't get a tree, he thought with some relief. What had she been thinking of? It'd be too late now to take a trip out to the pine plantation, and the shops would be well and truly closed. Ha!

Nevertheless, he was taking no chances. He spent more time than necessary doing a ward round, he ate dinner in the hospital kitchen—suppressing just the faintest niggle that Nell might have cooked something—and it was almost nine before he finally made his way home.

There was a tree in his sitting room!

It wasn't just a tree, he thought, stunned. It was the mother of all Christmas trees. She'd arranged her grandparents' furniture in a circle, there was a gorgeous Turkish rug in the centre of the room, and in a bucket in the centre of the rug was the pine plantation's biggest Christmas tree ever. It spread about eight feet in diameter, and its top just touched the ceiling. It dominated the room, its sweet scent of pine making him think of...

Of Christmas.

He'd blotted it out, he thought blankly. He hadn't thought of Christmas for years. Not properly. Christmas was a family day other people celebrated, while he spent it fixing up broken legs from new roller skates or coping with perforated ulcers from too much pudding.

Now, in the time it had taken to haul one massive tree into his home, Nell had hauled up all these memories that he'd successfully buried for years.

'Do you like it?' she demanded the minute he walked in the door, and he could only stop and blink.

'Um...'

'Isn't it huge?' She was on her knees, threading popcorn. 'Help me do this before Ernest gets the lot. I've had to repop four lots already.'

There was popcorn everywhere. Strands and strands of multicoloured corn were roped around the tree, and more was scattered on the rug. Ernest was in his basket where he'd obviously been banished, looking at the popcorn with mournful eyes.

'Here you go.' She rose stiffly to her feet and before he knew what she was about there was a threaded needle and a bowl of yellow corn in his hands. 'I'm off to dye some blue. Finish that, will you?'

He didn't seem to have any choice. He sat—and threaded popcorn.

'Where did you get the tree?' She had him fascinated. She'd been in town barely more than a day and she was organising faster than he'd thought possible.

'Lorna and Des Scott sent their son around to see if I needed any help.' She beamed. 'Wasn't that nice of them? I remember Des as the chemist when I was a little girl, and Ron's just like him. I met Lorna when I popped around to Ethel's this afternoon to see how she was getting on, and they couldn't have been more helpful. The pair of them were like two old chooks, planning our Christmas.'

He was having trouble taking this in, but one thing stood out. 'You popped around to Ethel's?'

'I was worried about her,' Nell told him, shaking her corn in its blue dye. 'She was so upset yesterday about breaking her diet that I thought a follow-through this afternoon wouldn't hurt. But don't worry. She's stuck to her diet all day and I found her reading recipe books and planning Christmas to her heart's content.'

Damn, he should have visited Ethel himself—but those sorts of things hadn't been done in Sandy Ridge. Follow-throughs. Unless they were urgent there simply hadn't been time.

With a jolt he realised that now there was. Follow-throughs... They were a medical imperative and now he'd have time to do them.

If they weren't done first by Nell.

'She was really OK?' he asked grudgingly, and she smiled.

'She was great. She was up to her elbows in mince pies, but she hadn't eaten a single one. She's talked to Mrs Condie and she's cooking them for the hospital patients. Oh, and for us.' She held up a tray of mince pies. 'I arrived just as a batch were coming out of the oven and they're delicious. Like one?'

'No. Thank you.'

It wasn't that he didn't want one. It was that he hardly dared have it. Sitting on the floor, threading Christmas decorations and eating mince pies... Things were starting to look seriously out of hand. He glanced at Ernest and found he was being regarded with a look that was suspiciously like sympathy.

'Does she organise you, too, boy?' he asked, and Nell glowered from the kitchen.

'Hey, I heard that.'

'Ernest wants some popcorn.'

'Ernest will pop himself if he eats anything more. He ate all my yellow corn while my back was turned. And it causes flatulence. He's sleeping on *your* bed tonight.'

'Spare room again, Ernest,' Blake told him, and grinned at the dopey dog's expression. Honestly, you'd swear he understood. He was one crazy dog. 'Where did you get him?'

'Who, Ernest?'

'That's who I mean.'

'Why do you ask?' Nell had gone back to corn-popping. She was holding the lid of the pot tight and the sound of popping corn filled the room.

'It's just... He seems ancient.'

'He was born ancient.'

'How old is he?'

'The vet thinks about twelve.'

'So you've had him for twelve years?'

'Nope.' She set her pot aside and returned to kneel under the tree. Picking up the corn, she also started threading, so they were side by side, threading in unison. It was a strange feeling. Intimate... 'I said the vet *thinks*,' she told him. 'If I'd had him since a puppy surely I'd know the age of my very own dog.'

'OK.' Her voice was cross and Blake found himself apologising. 'I'm sorry. Tell me how he came into your life.'

'I've only had him for a few months.'

'Really?' Blake's mouth twisted into laughter. 'Don't tell me. You went to the lost dogs' home and picked out the most decrepit one you could see.'

'There's no need to be rude about my dog.' She glowered. 'As a matter of fact, he chose me.'

'How?'

'It's a long story.'

'So I'm threading popcorn. I have all the time in the world.'

She hesitated and for a minute he thought she wouldn't go on. And then she shrugged. 'I was walking home from the hospital late at night and I was mugged. A group of four or five kids came from nowhere and grabbed me from behind. They hit me.' Her voice faded a bit. 'And…well, they took my bag and they hurt me. Not rape or anything, but they bashed… Anyway, when I finally figured out what was going on I was lying in the street, and Ernest was there. He was licking my face.'

Blake thought it through and watched her face. There was a heap going on here that he didn't understand and it behoved him to step carefully. 'Licking appears to be Ernest's specialty,' he said at last, and was rewarded with a smile.

'It is, isn't it?'

'I thought you were going to say he chased off the attackers.'

'Hey, there were five of them. Ernest had more sense. He knew the best course of action was to stay in the shadows and administer first aid.'

'And then what happened?' His eyes were still locked on Nell's. For some reason he found himself holding his breath. It was a sort of watershed, he realised. A chink in her armour. Maybe she'd finally tell him something.

'So I sat in the gutter and I howled and I howled, like a

great big sook. But I howled out a lot of stuff that had nothing to do with the mugging. I held onto Ernest and he licked me—and then I made a few resolutions.'

'I see.' The thought of her bashed filled his consciousness. Nell, sitting in the gutter, bleeding maybe, and sobbing... The image was light years away from the confident young woman he saw before him. It was jarring to say the least.

He didn't like the image at all. He found he was sitting by her Christmas tree with his hands clenching over fistfuls of popcorn—anger building at five unknown youths who'd dared to hurt her.

But she was no longer a victim. Not Nell. 'You don't see at all,' she said, a tiny smile flickering back. 'It was logical. I figured that was the end of me being a doormat. From that moment on, Ernest and I were going to take charge of our lives.'

He smiled up at her, and once again their eyes met. An unspoken message passed between them, and in that instant something changed. Something he couldn't define. But it was...nice. 'Well, bully for you and Ernest,' he told her gently, and she smiled.

'It is, isn't it?' Her beam returned in full. 'For one stray dog and one wimpish doctor we've done very well for ourselves. So maybe I should even be grateful to my muggers. Now...how's that popcorn going? Nearly threaded?'

'No. I—'

'Well, hurry up. There's more here.' And then she frowned. 'You did eat, by the way?'

'I ate over at the hospital.'

'Really?' She sounded as if she thought he was a dope for doing such a thing. 'Ernest and I made chicken pie. And chocolate pudding.'

He'd had cold mutton and salad. Damn.

Maybe he *was* a dope.

Maybe he didn't know what the hell he was any more.

So he sat and threaded popcorn, because that was all he could think of to do.

The nights were the longest. Would he ever be able to close his eyes at eleven and wake at seven with eight hours' uninterrupted sleep? Blake lay in the darkness, listening to a rising wind. His hands were linked behind his head and he stared up into the night with all the old familiar demons doing their haunting.

Curiously, though, tonight they were changed. Different.

He could still see Sylvia's face. That'd stay with him for ever. But tonight he wasn't seeing her as he'd seen her at the end. He was watching her as he'd first noticed her. At Christmas...

'Not the orange ones. You dingbat, can't you see I have a pink and white theme?' Her gorgeous face had laughed down at him from the ladder as she'd attached baubles to the ward Christmas tree. 'Yes, that's lovely,' she'd approved. 'Now, just stand there and hand them up, there's a lamb. But nothing that clashes.'

Sylvia would have hated Nell's tree, Blake thought. There wasn't a thing on the branches that went with anything else. It was a garish, outlandish jumble of everything she'd been able to scramble together.

'Well, you don't seem to have boxes of Christmas decorations lying around and I don't have cash to splash,' Nell had told him when he'd fingered the decorations in amazement. 'So a girl's got to do what a girl's got to do.'

What a girl had to do had stunned him. She'd fetched his waiting room's collection of magazines to the apartment and she'd ripped them into pieces. Now they were reassembled as masses of paper chains, looping through her threaded popcorn, and she'd made scores and scores of tiny paper lanterns to hang all over.

'Look,' she'd said, laughing and motioning to the highest

lantern. 'This one's a lantern made with Brad Pitt's six-pack. What a way to make a Christmas lamp.'

He grinned into the night at the thought of it.

But Sylvia would have had a fit.

Damn Sylvia.

The thought came from nowhere, astounding him. It was the first time he'd thought it. Up until now the guilt had been all-consuming. But now...

It was a great Christmas tree, he decided, and then he gave the image of his dead wife a grimace. 'Don't you spoil it for me.' As she'd spoiled everything else...

He sat up and flicked on the light, as he'd done every night now for over three years. But now it wasn't Sylvia he was thinking of.

The top of the tree was bare.

'We need an angel,' Nell had said sadly just before they'd retired for the night. She'd stood back and stared at the tree's tip with regret. 'We'll never find one now. I'd splash out and buy something as important as an angel, but the shops will have sold out long ago.'

And now, in the dark, a memory crept back—a long-ago memory from when he'd been about five years old. Back to kindergarten days.

'Fold here. Now cut. See, if you leave just a little bit on either wing, they'll join.' He'd made paper angels. Chains of paper angels.

They'd run out of paper.

He stared down at his bedside and his medical journals mocked him. Hmm. He could but try.

It was four in the morning. Nell had slept for five hours, but then she woke. The surf was starting to crash in the rising wind, and junior was kicking in no uncertain terms.

'Cornelius,' she threatened, but it was no good. Cornelius or Brunhilda kicked on. Finally she sighed, threw back the covers and emerged to the living room.

There were angels circling the top of her tree.

For a moment she thought she was dreaming, but then she looked again.

Blake had cut them with care. These were kindergarten angels cut by a man who'd trained as a surgeon. You could see the skill of surgeon's fingers in the way he'd cut the gorgeously intricate wings.

They were identical—well, they would be as he'd folded the pages into three and cut them as a chain. Then he'd joined the wing of the first and the third to form a ring. Now the ring of winged angels circled the tip of pine, and they beamed down...

How had he done the faces? How had he made them smile?

He'd cut them! The deep green of the tree made the intricate cuts in the glossy paper stand out as beaming smiles. Wondrous smiles. Smiles of blessing...

Nell stood back, stunned. They really were very, very good, and they completed her Christmas tree magnificently.

But he'd cut them from his medical journals.

There was an advertisement for haemorrhoid cream running around the base of the first angel!

Haemorrhoid cream advertisements on Christmas angels?

He was a nut, she thought, and found herself giggling. A nice nut. Underneath that grumpy, repellent shell she was starting to discover a very nice person.

She'd just have to struggle to expose it.

Which posed a dilemma. Why would you bother exposing anything? she asked herself. You're not interested in men.

It's just I'm interested in him as a person, she said to herself defensively. Not as a male.

Yeah, right. You dope, Nell.

I'm not a dope. I know what I'm doing. I can take care of myself.

Maybe she needed to go back to bed and stop thinking about it. Hmm.

The phone went at six, blasting through the sounds of wind and surf and waking both doctors. The hospital staff had been told to ring Blake again during the night, and the phone was by his bed, but Nell heard it. She'd left her door wide open and she saw him as he walked out of the bedroom, still talking on the mobile handset.

Well, why wouldn't she look? He was only wearing pyjama pants, and there was that chest again...

For heaven's sake, Nell McKenzie, she told herself as he flicked on the living room light and his body was clearly delineated in the frame of her bedroom door. Get a grip! And listening to him, her concentration on his chest faded immediately. She did indeed get a grip.

'How many? Right. You've contacted the ambulance? What about the coastguard?'

That was enough. Nell's covers were thrust aside and she padded out fast to see what was going on.

Ernest was there, too, awake and alert and looking only slightly hungry. Woman and dog stood beside the Christmas tree, and waited for Blake to finish. Blake's voice was curt and incisive, but mostly he listened.

'Yeah. Right. OK. Tell the ambulance to pick me up in two minutes. You might be able to winch me down from the top.'

And then he clicked off the receiver and headed back to his bedroom. Leaving the door open, he was throwing on his clothes regardless of the fact that Nell was standing by his bedroom door. He simply didn't notice.

This, then, was real trouble.

'Is there anything I can do?' Nell asked.

'No.' That was to the point. He was zipping his trousers and hauling on his shirt almost in one motion.

'What's happened?'

'A group of locals fishing from the clifftop.' He shoved his shirt into his trousers and reached for a sweater. 'Damn fools. They know these cliffs are unstable.'

'There's been a slide?'

That made him frown. He'd forgotten she was a local. She'd know what the problem was. The sandstone cliffs were notoriously unstable here, yet time and time again he'd seen fishermen edge closer to get their cast to land inches further out into the surf.

'Yes.'

'To be out in this wind…' She thought fast and knew they'd have selected this morning especially. With the wind behind them they could cast their lines further out to where the fish ran. 'How many fell?'

'Three. One's in the water. The coastguard's on the way, but God help him. Two are stuck on a ledge halfway down and one seems badly hurt.'

'I'll come.'

'You're seven months pregnant,' he said explosively. 'You'll only be in the way.'

And that was that. He hauled his sweater over his head, grabbed his boots and headed for the door.

CHAPTER FIVE

'YOU'LL only be in the way.' How often had she heard that? All her life, Nell thought bitterly, and it made no more sense now than it had all those years ago. 'Get out of my kitchen. Leave your grandfather alone. Go to your bedroom, Eleanor.'

'Why?'

'You're in the way.'

That statement was now a red rag to a bull, Nell decided as she hauled on her clothes. Damn the man! Who did he think he was?

'These are my people,' she told Ernest fiercely. 'I was brought up here. If there's fishermen stuck on the cliffs or in the water then I'll have known them for ever, and I'm trained in emergency medicine.'

Ernest looked at her with understanding, and as she raced to the door he sniffed after her.

'Sorry, boy,' she told him, not without irony. 'Not today. Believe it or not, you'd only be in the way.'

Someone—whoever had phoned—had obviously collected Blake. Nell had heard their vehicle accelerate away while she'd been throwing on her clothes—the same purple over-alls Blake had first seen her in. They might be flamboyant but they were practical. Now she emerged to the windswept dawn to find no one.

The hospital residence was on a bluff overlooking the town and the wind across the bluff almost blasted her side-ways.

The fishermen must be on the north cliffs, she decided as she headed for her car. They must be. At this time of year the tailor—a popular eating fish—would be running and the fishermen would be casting off the cliffs north of the river mouth. The cliffs were forty feet high, they were known to be dangerous and she knew about twenty men in the town who'd be stupid enough to fish there.

So she knew where to go. No thanks to Blake.

'Damn the man,' she muttered under her breath as she steered her Volkswagen northwards. 'Who does he think he is?'

He thought he was a hero!

Nell pulled up on the clifftop, parking well back from the ambulance and other vehicles. There was a cluster of men gathered where the cliff dropped to the sea, and as she climbed from her car she caught sight of Blake's dark sweater and gold-brown hair. He appeared to be sitting on the cliff edge.

He wasn't just sitting. As she ran closer she saw that he was in a harness, and as she watched in horror, he was lowered over the face of the cliff. Her breath caught in fear but she was too late. He was gone.

'What the hell do you think you're doing?'

Nell's barked command had men turning toward her. She was striding toward the cliff with a fierceness born of fear, and the wind was tearing at her back, almost pushing her out to sea. She had to raise her voice to be heard above wind and surf.

'Of all the stupid… Look how close you are! Will you get back?' There were six of them standing right on the edge. 'If the edge has crumbled already, don't you realise it can go again? Bring Dr Sutherland back up. Now!'

'We can't do it, Nell,' one of the fishermen said dully, turning back to stare down the cliff with eyes that had room for only one thing. 'The only other way to reach them is with a helicopter and we can't wait. Tom's down there, and Dan, and Dan can't breathe. Tom yelled up that he was turning blue. He's unconscious and there's blood coming out of his mouth, so it was send the doc over or have him die before we could reach him.'

Nell was forced to leave Blake on the ledge. A man could be dying of airway obstruction. Blake had gone down because he could focus on only one thing, so it was up to her to focus on others—like getting these fools back from the cliff edge before Blake ended up with more patients down there.

'Where's the fire chief?' she snapped. When she'd left town twelve years ago the fire chief had been the man to turn to in emergencies. Allan had a fierce intellect, enough courage for a small army and, in times of drama, there was no one she'd rather rely on.

'He's in Brisbane for his daughter's wedding,' one of the men said helplessly, and Nell realised with a sinking heart that the trouble with having someone so competent in charge was the void it left with him gone.

And all the men were looking at her. Good grief! Ten years ago the townsfolk had looked at her like she was a scrap of an unwanted kid. Now, because she'd raised her voice in anger and because she was deemed a doctor, she was looked to for answers.

And of all the fishermen in the town, these were the stupidest. So the void had to be filled by her.

'OK, move back,' she told them. 'Now!' The rope they were holding had gone slack. Blake had presumably reached his ledge. Then, once the rest of the men were back from the edge, she ventured forward herself, crawling on all fours to see.

Yes, Blake had reached the ledge. A rocky outcrop fifteen feet down had caught the two men. Blake was there now, crouched over a prone figure while another watched with helpless dismay.

It was better than she'd dared hope. The ledge seemed solid. A mass of loose dirt seemed to have come from the top when it had crumbled, but the ledge itself looked as if it might hold.

She stayed where she was, lying on her stomach—with difficulty because of her pregnancy—and watched what Blake was doing. The way Blake was moving, she could tell that every ounce of his concentration was on the injured man. If Dan was dying of airway obstruction, it'd take every bit of Blake's skill to keep him alive in such a situation.

'Is Blake carrying his phone?'

'There's no reception out here,' someone told her, and she bit her lip. Damn.

OK, she had to think for herself—and for Blake. She couldn't yell down to him. From where she was he probably wouldn't hear and it was too dangerous to lean right over.

'Right.' She inched back and stood up, walking away from the edge and pushing into the wind as she gazed swiftly around the remaining men. Three fishermen, two fire officers and one ambulance officer. She knew them all.

'Bill, you inch forward and take my place,' she ordered. 'Stay on your stomach and put your weight as far back as you can.' Then she explained her reasons to the others. 'We need someone to direct the winch, and Bill's the only one whose family are grown.'

They saw the sense in that. If anyone had to risk their life, it should be someone without dependants. 'OK by me,' Bill said grimly.

'Blake'll need oxygen,' Nell told them. She'd seen that he'd carried his doctor's bag down with him—he therefore had the means to do an emergency tracheotomy if he must—but he'd had no time to organise more. She didn't want Blake wasting time now, calling up directions and waiting for equipment. She turned to the ambulance officer. 'Henry, do you have a portable oxygen cylinder in the ambulance?'

'Sure thing, Nell. I mean Doc…'

'Give it to Bill before he goes close to the edge. And give him another rope. The fewer trips he has to make back and forth to the edge, the safer it'll be. Send saline solution down, too, and the things Blake needs to set up a drip.' She hesitated. 'Bill, are you sure you're OK with this? I can do it if you can't.'

'You can't,' Bill said heavily. 'You've got a littly on board. Have a bit of sense, Doc.'

She nodded, but in her mind she'd already moved on. Apart from supplying Blake with equipment, if Bill was willing to stay by the edge there was little more she could do here. So triage… Move to the next priority. They'd said there were three men.

'The man who fell into the water…'

'The coastguard's reached him.' One of the men gave a rueful grimace. 'Their boat was out already—well, it would be if the fish are running, 'cause they always do a bit of fishing on the side—and they saw what happened. They damn near splintered their boat on the cliffs, getting him aboard, but they did it. But he looked unconscious when they hauled him in.'

'And now?' Nell looked out over the white-capped sea but she couldn't see the brilliant orange of the coastguard vessel. 'Where's the boat now?'

'It's taking him back to harbour.' The fisherman hesitated. 'Dunno if they'll get in until the tide turns, though, but they're going to try.'

'I'll go down to meet them,' Nell told them. She didn't want to. She felt sick to the stomach at the idea of leaving Blake in these incapable hands—of leaving three men stuck on the crumbling cliff face—but there was an injured man being brought back into harbour who could well need her services more.

What else was needed here? The men were looking at her in helpless dismay and she wanted to knock a few heads together.

'Get more men out here,' she ordered. 'I want the fire crew.' Surely if the whole fire crew arrived there'd be someone with more intelligence than this lot. 'But don't let anyone but Bill go near the edge. Get long planking laid between here and the edge so when you're winching equipment, the pressure's not on the absolute edge. And, for heaven's sake, wait for the helicopter to bring the men up. If you try and take their weight from here…'

She didn't need to say more. The fear was in her voice and it was reflected in all their faces.

Oh, Blake, she thought as she ran back toward her car. She stopped at the ambulance and grabbed a few things she thought she might need herself.

She should be praying for all of them, she thought. She was. But mostly she was praying for Blake. She'd only known him for two days. The way she was feeling didn't make sense but, sense or not, that was the way it was.

A sudden image of Blake's paper angels sprang to mind. As she turned her car down toward the harbour she felt tears stinging at the back of her eyes. 'You look after him,' she commanded, and it was a direct order to his three paper angels, their crazy haemorrhoid cream included.

'Dear God…' Things weren't destined to get any easier. Nell pulled up at the jetty and what she saw made her feel sick all over again.

'The tide… Oh, no…'

Sandy Ridge harbour was formed by a river mouth, and behind the town the river broadened into a massive tidal lake. Tides were, to say the least, impressive. The water movement was massive.

Local fishing boats would normally wait until ebb tide before attempting to come back into harbour. To attempt anything else in weather like this was almost suicidal. As she pulled up, she could see waves breaking over the rocky entrance. Help!

And then she saw a face she knew. 'Grace!' Here, at last, was someone who was capable of sharing responsibilities.

Grace Mayne had fished with her father and then her husband since she was ten years old. She was now well into her eighties, she was fiercely intelligent and if anyone could help Nell it was Grace.

The old woman had been standing on the jetty, eyeing the harbour mouth with disfavour. She turned to Nell as she approached, gave her a flicker of a welcoming—and assessing—look and then went back to staring at the sea.

'The coastguard boat…' Nell managed.

'We've heard.' Grace didn't turn back as Nell reached her. She was staring out to sea with eyes that had seen it all. In her dingy overalls, with her weathered skin and her washed-out green eyes and faded copper hair, the old lady seemed almost a part of the sea itself. 'The coastguard radioed in to say they picked up Aaron Gunner. He's in a pretty bad way, but they can't get in. Not yet. They'd be pushing against the tide with the water breaking forward. I wouldn't try right now. No one would.'

'How long?'

'It'll be a good two hours before the ebb.'

'Do they say what's wrong with Aaron?'

Grace nodded. 'Leg's a mess. Bone sticking through the skin. Bleeding like a stuck pig. He was unconscious when they hauled him out of the water but he's coming round now. Screaming, they say.'

Dear God…

'The chopper's coming from Sydney,' Grace told her. 'Marion's been on the radio to the ambulance, trying to find out what's going on, because Doc Sutherland's phone's out of range. The ambulance boys told her you were coming here. She said to tell you the chopper'll be an hour or maybe a bit longer, but they'll need it for the men on the cliff first.'

Grace paused and surveyed Nell's face with care. 'Looks like Aaron mightn't make it?' And it wasn't a statement. It was a question.

'Mmm.'

Silence. Nell shaded her eyes and both women stared out to the river mouth. There was a wash of white water, almost like rapids, bursting out toward the open sea. To try and fight that current to bring a boat in... Impossible!

But maybe there was another way. The tidal flow seemed at maximum so the surge of water outward was massive, stronger than the incoming rush of breakers. Nell turned to Grace, a sudden flare of hope in her eyes.

'Grace, I know getting into harbour's impossible, but could you get me out?'

Grace stared. 'What, through that?'

'I remember you fought a tide like this a few years back,' Nell told her, and managed a smile. 'Mind, that was a real emergency. There was a bushfire, the road was cut off and the town was out of beer. Half the fleet took off for Bay Beach.'

'Wasn't like this, though.' Grace went back to assessing the river mouth. 'It was later. The flow wasn't as strong and there wasn't as much wind.' She wrinkled her already massively wrinkled face. 'Going out now'd be like riding the rapids.'

'But we'd be going with the flow of the water.'

'We?'

'I want you to take me out there,' Nell said urgently. 'Can you do it?'

'But—'

'You know I'm a doctor.'

'Yeah. Just like your grandpa.' But Grace's eyes narrowed. 'Though maybe not like your grandpa if you want to take these sort of crazy risks for Aaron.' She took a deep breath. 'I'm eighty-three,' she said at last. 'Everybody I care for's dead. It doesn't matter if I go down with the boat. But you've got a baby aboard.'

'And I'll bet Aaron has a family.'

'He has,' Grace said grudgingly. 'Three littlies. Nice wife. Stupid, but nice.'

'There you go, then.' Nell swung back to her car. 'I'll grab some equipment and then let's go.'

'You're mad,' Grace told her, but she was speaking to no

one. Nell was heading for her car, and for a long moment Grace stared after her.

There were more fishing boats lined up on the wharf. If she didn't take Nell, Nell would persuade someone else to take her, she thought.

What had she told the girl? *Everybody I care for's dead.* It wasn't quite true. Not now.

With a sigh Grace climbed aboard her boat—and then she grinned, the dreary blanket of depression that had been hovering over her since the death of her husband lifting like magic. 'We're both mad,' she muttered. 'But who dares wins. Right?' She chuckled as Nell came running back with her equipment. 'Welcome to town, Dr McKenzie. We're very pleased to see you home.'

In the end they didn't do it alone. As soon as Grace gunned her motor they had every fisherman not already at sea rushing to their boatside.

'What the hell do you think you're doing?'

'You know Aaron's dying and they can't get him into the harbour,' Grace said curtly, motioning to Nell who was storing equipment in the cabin. 'So we're going out. I'm taking Dr McKenzie out to see if there's something she can do.'

'Not alone, you're not' was the consensus, and when they finally slipped their moorings they had a crew of four. All of them were as old as Grace or older, but they had no intention of taking unnecessary risks. Each of them was weighed down with safety gear.

'Because we might be old but we're still good for a few years yet,' the ancient fishermen told Nell, grinning at her as they slipped through the last patch of calm water. 'Between us we must have more than three hundred years of seagoing experience. Let's hope some of it pays off.'

They told Blake what was happening and he nearly had them winch him up straight away.

'They radioed from the harbour,' Bill told him from the clifftop. The wind had eased just a bit—enough for them to hear themselves speak. 'Grace Mayne has taken her boat out to meet the coastguard, and she's taken Nell with her.'

'Through the outgoing tide?' Blake's voice was incredulous. 'In these conditions?' They had to be mad.

'Yeah.' Bill sounded as sick as Blake felt. 'Can't say I like it.'

Like it? The man was a moron. Blake turned back to his patient and it was just as well the fisherman took most of his attention or he would have gone crazy. Once more he checked on Dan's airway, clearing the blood that filled his mouth almost as soon as he swabbed it away. He had Dan lying on his side. The blood came from fractured teeth that had torn his gums. It wasn't life-threatening—as long as Blake concentrated—but Bill's news made that almost impossible.

Damn the woman. She was pregnant, for heaven's sake!

She'd gone out with Grace… And Grace was suicidal. He knew it. The elderly woman had told him so herself. She was refusing to take antidepressants, and here she was, pushing her boat at something that was likely to kill her. And she wouldn't care.

She'd take Nell with her.

The thought was savagely, piercingly dreadful. He felt sick, so much so that the other fisherman on the ledge leaned toward him with concern. 'You all right, Doc?'

He caught himself. 'Yeah. Never better,' he muttered, and reached for another swab.

Dear God. Nell…

Which was pretty much exactly what Nell was thinking. Crossing the harbour entrance was the most hair-raising thing she'd done in her life. It was white-water rafting at its most dangerous—not on a raft, but on a bathtub of an ancient fishing boat. All the decent boats with more powerful motors were already at sea, so it was Grace's ancient tub or nothing.

Nell was strapped into a lifejacket, clipped to a lifeline and told to stay put.

'You're under orders,' Grace yelled at her as one of the fishermen helped her fasten herself her onto the sheets. 'If the boat rolls, then you undo that clip. Fast. The line'll keep you safe while we're upright, but if the boat goes under then it'll tie you there. You'll drown.'

'Gee, thanks…'

They all had clips. They might be ancient and they might also be desperate to help, but they were taking minimal chances. Grace was taking minimal chances. She was using every ounce of skill she possessed to keep the boat safe.

She was wonderful, Nell thought. Her geriatric saviour!

And then they hit white water, and Nell thought of nothing but keeping alive.

There was water all around her. The mass of water rushing out of the harbour was so great that it was seething into the stern of the boat. There were waves breaking in front of them, creating eddies and whirlpools like something out of a nightmare.

It was a pretty wet nightmare! Maybe there was a better metaphor but she couldn't see it. In fact, after the first rush of white water she couldn't see anything at all. She was soaked and she was blinded and she was concentrating only on each sodden breath.

'Go to it, Grace,' she prayed over and over. But it wasn't just Grace. There were three of them on the wheel, using their combined strength to hold the boat on course and stopping it slamming into the harbour wall. The other fisherman was monitoring the pumps, and it was only Nell who stood uselessly where she'd been clipped.

'You'd only get in the way,' Grace told her when she'd wanted to help, and she'd grimaced.

That's what Blake had said to her, and they were her grandmother's words, echoing down through the years.

But this time it was different. This time she knew it was true. Grace knew her boat and she didn't, and it'd be little use to anyone if they managed to get through the harbour mouth only to have the doctor they were carrying washed overboard. So Nell accepted her role of idleness, but she felt very small and very vulnerable and, to be honest, she also felt very, very afraid.

For the first time she wondered whether this was fair on her unborn baby, and she knew it wasn't. She'd raced into it without thinking. They advised pregnant women to give up smoking because of the threat to the unborn child, but this... How much greater threat was this?

She put her hand protectively on her stomach.

'If I get through this I'll never threaten you with Cornelius or Brunhilda again,' she whispered to her little one. 'I promise.'

She hoped to God it was enough.

And then they were through. The last rush of water shoved them forward like a cork from a bottle, and they emerged to sunshine and water that was rough but, compared to what they'd just been through, it was like a mill pond. Nell gasped and wiped water from her eyes and then proceeded to count heads. Her four wonderful geriatrics were all beaming at her like they'd won the pools.

'Who said only the youngies know how to handle a boat?' Grace chortled. 'Well done, us.' Her eyes rested on Nell for a moment, her old eyes meeting Nell's young ones in a flash of triumphant recognition. Then it was back to business. 'Adam, how much water do we have on board?'

'Don't take on any more,' Adam advised. 'A sparrow lands on this deck and we're under.' But the pumps were going full throttle, spurting the water out behind them, and for now things could only get better.

They had to find the coastguard boat with the crew and Aaron.

'They tried to come into harbour but when they couldn't they went back to the shelter of the north cliffs,' Grace told her. She'd left the wheel to one of the others and had checked the radio. 'It's calmer there and they're standing off far enough to keep from getting pounded on the rocks. But Aaron sounds…' She faltered, and this time her eyes didn't meet Nell's. 'Well, he's lost consciousness again and they can't stop the bleeding. I hope to hell we haven't come this far for nothing.'

She was there. Grace's old tub of a boat rounded the headland and Blake nearly stood up and cheered. He counted heads. There were five on board and he could see Nell's crazy patchwork overalls from here. Bless the overalls. He hadn't realised how much he loved them.

Loved them? Liked, he corrected himself, and suddenly it mattered to him that he did. Liked. That's what he did. He didn't do love. Nell was a competent doctor; she was working alongside him and he owed her a responsibility. That's why he'd felt sick—nothing more.

Under his hands Dan stirred and moaned and Blake adjusted his air-flow. 'Take it easy, mate,' he murmured, but it wasn't quite a murmur. There was jubilation in his voice, and he felt like a kid who'd been handed a Santa sack all for himself.

The men on the coastguard boat watched the geriatric crew approach with amazement, and when they saw Nell there was even more amazement.

She must look a real sight, Nell thought ruefully—a half-drowned doctor, very pregnant, wearing soaking purple patchwork. But she had work to do. There was no time to think about her appearance.

She sorted equipment to be taken on board and then, finally, she allowed herself one uneasy glance up the cliff face. Only one. She shouldn't even take that. There was nothing for her to do even if Blake had fallen. It was the first rule of medicine in an emergency to not allow oneself to be distracted by things you could do nothing about, but…

Please, God. Protect Blake…

And blessedly, joyously, he was still there. He was still crouched over the injured fisherman, and that had to be a good sign. It meant his patient was alive, and there hadn't been a further fall.

But from underneath, the ledge didn't look nearly as solid as it had from up top. In fact, from here the ledge looked as if it could give way at any minute.

'Don't think about it,' she told herself fiercely. 'Triage, Dr McKenzie. Concentrate on what's important.'

Which was Aaron, not Blake! Thinking of Blake only led to trouble—in more ways than one.

And Aaron certainly needed her.

Her transfer from boat to boat, tricky at the best of times, was achieved with Nell hardly thinking about it. She couldn't. Her mind was already assessing what needed to be done. She took one look at the man lying on the deck and her heart sank. Back at Sydney Central she'd have had him in Theatre in minutes. She'd have had blood banks on the line, she'd have been cross-matching, she'd have had surgeons and…

Well, here she had herself and only herself, and she was already kneeling beside him as her equipment was transferred after her.

'Good luck,' Grace called as the boats pulled apart, and Nell knew that she was going to need it.

What she needed, in fact, was Blake—or at least another doctor—but she was all she had.

Nell did a fast assessment which was harder than she'd thought on the rolling boat. There was no head wound. The lack of consciousness must be due to shock and loss of blood, she thought. The fracture was compound, and it bled sluggishly even though the coastguard crew had tied the upper leg with a tourniquet. And that couldn't stay there. Nell felt his foot and flinched at the coldness of it. Soon he'd have tissue death.

Or complete death. How much blood had he lost? The deck was awash with it.

The first thing to do was to stop the bleeding. There must be a severed artery. 'There's antiseptic in my bag. Do you have any more?' Heck, she needed antiseptic by the bucket load. To tie off an artery in these conditions… She had no choice.

'There's a light in the bag. I want it held straight down at his leg,' she ordered, shoving her bag into someone's hands as she applied a fist to the pressure point above the wound. 'And I want fishing line.'

She was thinking fast as she ripped Aaron's already shredded trouser leg. 'You.' She picked a random man of the half-dozen clustered around. 'Hold yourself steady against the rail and hold the plasma. Don't move. And, you… Kneel here and take over. See where I'm pressing? I want you to do the same.'

She worked swiftly and incisively, her training allowing her to almost forget her surroundings. She'd used human dripstands before. This was the stuff Nell was trained to do. As doctor in charge of a busy city casualty ward—and at the scene of accidents when needed—she'd been at the coal face time and time again. When patients had been stuck in damaged cars and couldn't be shifted, she'd been able to cope.

She'd had back-up there, though, she thought. Trained ambulance crew. Paramedics. But here… Here there was no one. And Blake was still on that dreadful ledge.

Don't think of Blake! Think of what she needed to do.

She'd only brought four units of plasma, she thought grimly as she searched through the damaged flesh, trying to locate the artery. Four units didn't look nearly enough. And where was the artery?

Ah, there it was, under her fingers, still spurting blood despite the tourniquet. She had no choice but to tie it off, even though it might mean losing the foot.

The foot might be the least of Aaron's troubles. She used

fishing line to tie off the artery and allowed herself a few
deep breaths. Then…

'When did you say the helicopter'll be here?'

'Maybe an hour.'

An hour! Help.

'Does anyone here know their blood group?' she demanded. It was a forlorn hope, but she had to ask. 'There
isn't anyone with O-negative blood, is there?' O-negative
was the universal donor. Without the facilities to cross-
match, that was her only hope. Or Aaron's only hope.

And amazingly there was. Two men—brothers by the
look of them.

'We're blood donors,' they told her. 'Doc Sutherland uses
us a lot. Because, yep, we're O-negative.'

Miracle of miracles. O-negative and blood donors… If
Blake used them regularly she could assume their blood was
safe. Another glance at Aaron's deathly white face confirmed
what she believed. He was unconscious and he'd lost so
much blood there was a risk of brain damage. The extra
risks from not cross-checking would be more than out-
weighed by Aaron's increased chances of survival.

But could she do a blood transfusion on this heaving boat?
She did a frantic visual check of equipment, thought it
through and then nodded. She could but try. She had no
choice.

'OK. Lie down and swab your arms with antiseptic,' she
told them. 'As soon as I have this bleeding stopped, I'll be
using you. I need all the blood I can get.'

Her confidence silenced them all. The men were staring
at her in amazement. These were local men and they knew
her—or they'd thought they knew her. This was Nell
McKenzie. Nell! The sad little town girl who'd been more
trouble than she'd been worth.

'Just do it,' she said, sensing their uncertainty. 'You need
to trust me.'

They looked again—and then both her potential blood donors nodded. Trust her? They did.

                    *   *   *

The helicopter finally came from the north, and Nell was never more pleased to see anything in her life. By that time her major anxiety was for Blake and the other two men trapped on the ledge.

She'd done all she could for Aaron. He desperately needed surgery if they were to save his leg, but she'd stopped the bleeding and given him enough blood to avoid brain damage. Or more brain damage. She'd feel a whole lot better if he gained consciousness. But now there was nothing else for her to do but to gaze up to where the ledge looked more and more fragile every time she looked. To Blake.

But then the helicopter appeared. The men and women on board were competent and professional. They swung in over the cliff, a stretcher was lowered and within ten minutes everyone on the ledge had been winched to the top. Blake was winched up last, and as Nell saw him being hauled upward she felt almost sick with relief.

Then there was a brief pause when they landed on the clifftop, followed by the wail of the ambulance siren receding into the distance. Presumably Blake and the injured fisherman were on their way to hospital. Nell could finally let out her breath on Blake's behalf. Dear God, thank you.

Why had she felt sick? She hardly knew the man. She'd met him two days ago. It didn't make sense. She was accustomed to trauma—why should Blake's fate worry her more than others?

She only knew that it did. It wasn't sensible in the least—but still it did.

Then it was their turn. The chopper was back, lowering a stretcher for Aaron. It was a tricky operation on the choppy sea but this crew was good! Two paramedics were lowered as well. It hadn't been safe to lower anyone not absolutely essential onto the ledge, but onto the boat it was different. Nell was suddenly redundant in the face of these people's far superior training in moving the injured.

'We'll take him straight to the hospital,' the paramedics

told her, strapping Aaron onto the stretcher with skill and speed. 'The chopper should reach the hospital almost as soon as the ambulance, and your Dr Sutherland will be there to meet him.'

Her Dr Sutherland... The thought brought an unexpected jolt of comfort. She didn't understand why, but it did.

Finally, the winch was lowered once more. 'This time it's you, Doc,' the paramedics told her. 'It'll be more than an hour before the boat can get you into harbour. There'll be two patients back at the hospital now and Doc Sutherland needs help. He doesn't want to send either man to Blairglen—at least until they're stable—so he's asked us to bring you in.'

It made sense, Nell thought, but the idea of stepping into the harness and being winched upward made her feel ill. She had a baby on board.

She looked at the harness, saw that her weight wouldn't hang too heavily against her abdomen and shrugged.

'I'm really sorry, baby,' she whispered as she was roped into the harness. 'If we get through this I'll buy you the safest, snuggliest bassinet known to man, and I'll never put you at risk again. Promise.'

And then she was whisked up into the sky, to the chopper waiting overhead. To the hospital.

To Blake.

And it was a Blake who was seething.

'What the hell do you think you've been playing at?' Nell was no sooner through the door of Casualty than Blake's pent-up anxiety exploded into unreasonable fury. 'To go through the harbour mouth at that time. It was madness!'

But Nell wasn't in the mood for apologies. She was feeling sick with relief at being on firm ground, and she wanted to yell herself.

'You know I had no choice.' She took a deep breath and steadied. 'How's Dan?'

Her carefully produced matter-of-fact tone had its effect,

and only Nell herself knew how hard it had been to produce it. 'Stable.' Blake caught himself and grimaced. If she could act professionally then he'd better match it.

'He's broken his nose, smashed some teeth and knocked himself out. The combination almost killed him—he was breathing blood—but once I had an airway established he was fine. He's conscious now, his breathing's regular and I'm happy with him.'

'Right.' Nell was now purely in professional mode. In truth, the events of the morning had left her feeling dizzy, but there was work to do before she could indulge her own emotions. She couldn't afford to let herself be anything other than a doctor.

And she certainly couldn't afford to do what she wanted—which was to put her arms around this damned man and hug him senseless. She hadn't realised how frightened she'd been until then. Frightened for herself, frightened for her baby—frightened for Blake!

Frightened for Blake? Why should she have been more frightened for him than for anyone else on the ledge? Why was he making her think like that?

Medicine! Concentrate on medicine. And somehow she did. 'Then Aaron needs our attention first.' She motioned down to Aaron's gory leg. 'The leg fracture needs reducing.' She didn't explain further. Blake could see for himself what the problem was. The blood supply to the foot was almost completely blocked and the leg was flaccid and white.

'I've tied off an artery, and the compound fracture is obstructing what remains of his blood supply,' she told him. 'We need to straighten it enough to get blood through until he gets to a vascular surgeon.' She took a deep breath. 'He'll need to be taken to Blairglen for that, though.'

'I can do that—if you'll back me up with anaesthetic.'

She stared. Vascular surgery… 'You're kidding!'

He shrugged. 'Vascular surgery was my specialty. I've done very little since I moved here but I can do what's necessary.'

'Right.' She believed him. There was something about Blake Sutherland that said he wasn't a man to blow his own trumpet lightly. If he said he could do it, she wouldn't argue, and the time difference between operating now or waiting to operate until after transfer to the city might very well be the deciding factor in saving the foot.

She cast one long assessing look at Blake, and she made up her mind. Aaron was loaded with morphine and drifting in and out of consciousness, and she squeezed his hand. 'Aaron, can you hear us?'

There was a faint return of pressure on her fingers. Which was wonderful. If he was responding now, it meant that the possibility of brain damage through blood loss was minimal.

'That's terrific,' she said. Blake was watching her, the last traces of his anger fading in the face of her professionalism. 'Your leg's at an odd angle and it's blocking the blood supply to your foot,' she told him. 'Dr Sutherland and I are going to put you to sleep and straighten it out. Is that OK with you?'

Another squeeze.

'Well done,' she said gently. Then she looked through to the waiting area. 'I'm guessing that's your wife outside, waiting. Wendy, isn't it? I recognise her from school. We'll bring her in before we pop you to sleep.'

Then she moved back to Blake's side, out of Aaron's hearing, and she focussed on what lay ahead and only that. If she let herself feel exhaustion or let the terror of the morning take hold, she'd never get through this. 'You're sure you can do this?'

He was watching her face and he was concerned. 'If you're sure you can do the anaesthetic.'

'I don't see we have a choice. If this fracture's not reduced soon, he'll lose his foot. And I've done my first part anaesthetics. It's the major reason I had the job as senior casualty officer. I could put drips in better than anyone else in the hospital.'

And she, too, wasn't boasting. It was the simple truth, and Blake had the sense to recognise it.

He cast her one last long look, though, and she knew he was seeing past the professionalism to the tumult of emotions that lay beyond. Sensibly, however, he accepted that they had to be ignored.

'Then let's go,' he said. 'Together we can do this.' And he touched her lightly on the arm. 'Together...'

Finally they were finished. With Aaron in Recovery, Donald hovering by his side as the most competent attendant nurse they could wish for and Dan settled into the ward, there was time to stand back and take stock.

Not bad. Not bad at all, Nell decided. All that drama and no deaths.

But now that the need for action had passed, exhaustion washed over her like a heavy blanket. She ripped off her surgical gown and let it drop beside her. Suddenly she didn't have the energy to move it an inch further.

Blake was watching her. They'd been operating for over two hours, and he was almost as exhausted as Nell, but his eyes were only for her.

'Sit down,' he told her.

'I don't—'

'Sit down.' Before she knew what he was about he'd placed his hands on her shoulders and propelled her into a chair. 'You look like you're about to fall over.'

'I'm not—'

'Don't argue. You have every right to fall wherever you want.'

She looked up at him, stunned. Good grief! There was something in his voice that she hardly recognised. Tenderness? Surely not!

'That was a magnificent effort,' Blake told her, and this time there was no mistaking the emotion behind his voice. 'From start to finish it's been little short of miraculous. To tie off the artery… To do blood transfusions on board a boat in filthy weather. And that anaesthetic…'

After that amount of blood loss they really should have stabilised Aaron first, but it was operate immediately or have him lose his leg. And Nell pulled him through. 'Daniel told me you were good,' he said. 'But until now I hadn't realised just how good.'

She managed a smile. 'I try to please—and you're not bad yourself.' That was an understatement. His skill as a vascular surgeon had left her stunned.

But he wasn't listening. He was focussed on her. 'Hell, you're past exhaustion.'

'Maybe.' She wasn't about to commit herself any further.

'And I'll bet you're still wet from that damned boat.'

'I am not.' Somehow Nell raised a hint of indignation and a smile. 'Even my knickers are dry by now.' She lifted her legs out and her crazy overalls were as stiff as board before her. 'See? Dry as a bone, though I've got so much salt stuck to me…'

'And blood.' Blake was gazing down at her patchwork legs in disgust. 'And I can see—and smell—the odd fish scale or two. Plus, there's grease and antiseptic and heaven knows what else. I'm putting up Aaron's antibiotic level to maximum and then some.'

She could only agree, but she was too tired to care. Blake was in charge now. 'Mmm.'

He smiled. 'How about taking your wonderful overalls off and I'll get someone to take them to the cleaners? It'd be a shame to lose them.'

She blinked. 'My wonderful overalls?' Was she hearing right? 'Excuse me,' she said cautiously, 'but you don't like my overalls.'

'Who said I didn't?'

'I'm sure you didn't. Your face said you didn't.'

'Then my face said wrong,' he growled. 'There's nothing wrong with your overalls. In fact, there's nothing wrong with you.' He hesitated. 'Nell, if it wasn't for you, Aaron would

be dead now. And those no-hopers at the top of the cliff…
I told them to move back but they have the brains of sheep.
I was never more grateful for anything than when I heard
your voice.'

'Being bossy.'

'Bossy's great, especially when it means I don't have another couple of fool fishermen landing on my head.' He
smiled down at her—and such a smile! It made her catch
her breath in something akin to panic.

'I'll hold you to that,' she said, and if her voice was a
trifle unsteady, who could blame her? 'I… Maybe I'd best
see to Aaron and talk to his wife. He should be almost
awake.'

'I'll see to Aaron,' Blake told her. He smiled again, deep-
ening her sense of unreality. 'And then I'll do afternoon
surgery while you, Dr McKenzie, take off those disgusting
overalls, shower, get into bed and sleep. For the rest of the
day.'

'But—'

'No argument,' he told her firmly. 'Do you want to risk
losing your baby?'

That stopped Nell. Maybe she had done a bit much today,
she acknowledged. If anything happened to this pregnancy…
'No! I mean…of course I don't!'

'There you go, then,' he told her. 'Bed. Now! And you're
not to stir until I come and wake you.'

There was nothing more to be said. Except…

'Yes, sir,' she said meekly—and took herself off to bed.
And the caring in his voice stayed with her until she went
to sleep, and longer.

CHAPTER SIX

IT WAS nearly seven p.m. when Blake woke Nell. He was reluctant to wake her even then, but she hadn't eaten lunch. They'd operated straight through. Now there was no evidence to show him that she'd eaten anything before she'd fallen into bed.

Dinner was ready. Damn, he *was* a doctor, she *was* pregnant and she had to take care of herself, but when he opened her door a crack to discover she was still fast asleep, his reluctance deepened. Her hand was curled under her cheek and her bright splash of copper curls looked vivid against the stark white of the pillow. She looked like a child.

She was anything but a child, he thought, letting his mind drift through the morning's events. Her skills had stunned him. She was an amazing doctor.

She was an amazing woman.

She was his Christmas gift, he thought suddenly, and he was incredibly lucky to have her.

As was Aaron. Blake was under no illusions. If Nell hadn't been here this morning—if she hadn't taken the risks she had—Aaron would be dead and there'd be a wife and three children facing a dreadful Christmas. Instead, they'd have a Christmas with a grumpy fisherman with his leg in a cast, but it definitely beat the alternative.

Ernest was shifting on the foot of Nell's bed. He saw Blake and wriggled his rump, thumping his disreputable tail against Nell's legs so that Nell stirred and opened her eyes.

And she smiled. Dear heaven... That was some smile!

He was standing there like an inane fool. Somehow he

94

managed to give himself a mental shake and haul his thoughts back on track.

'Hi, sleepyhead. Are you hungry?'

'Oh…' It was a lovely, drawn-out sigh. She stretched out in her bed like a cat. 'Oh, I guess I am.' She glanced at her bedside clock and her eyes flew wide. 'Seven!'

'You've slept most of the afternoon. If you'd slept any longer it would have turned into morning, and I thought you should eat before settling for the night. For the sake of junior.'

'Junior hasn't been getting such a good deal lately,' she admitted ruefully, and sat up. And then, as the sheet fell away, she gasped and hauled her bedclothes hastily back against her. She'd fallen asleep stark naked. Blake had a glimpse of full and gorgeous breasts, and then she was covered again.

She didn't blush. Instead…she giggled!

'Whoops,' she said, and hauled her sheets tighter against her. 'Sorry. I couldn't find my nightie. I looked for a whole two seconds and then bed called so urgently I couldn't resist.'

'Don't mind me,' Blake managed, though only just, and her smile widened at his discomfort.

'I don't. Ernest thought it didn't matter, and seeing as he's the only man in my life…'

'Lucky Ernest.'

'He is, isn't he?' She gave her dog an enormous hug— and Blake had another glimpse of those breasts!

For heaven's sake! He was a doctor and she was a pregnant woman. The glimpse of a bit of breast shouldn't have the capacity to knock him sideways.

But it did.

He was tired, he told himself. That was all it was, nothing more. Make yourself talk sensibly, Sutherland. Now!

'Dinner's ready when you are.'

'Great.' She made to throw her covers off and then thought better of it. 'Whoops,' she said again. And grinned.

'I'm determined to be unrespectable. Sorry. Could you and Ernest please leave?'

'We know when we're not wanted.' Blake struggled to find a smile himself. Keep it light… He clicked his fingers. 'Come on, Ernest. The lady wants some privacy.'

She wasn't fooled for an instant. 'It's not me who's embarrassed,' Nell called as he beat a hasty retreat. 'Where's your professional detachment, Dr Sutherland?'

He didn't have any and he knew it. He and Ernest headed for the kitchen and closed the door, and it was all he could do not to lock it after him.

Dinner was steak, chips and salad—Blake's staple diet. Every evening he followed almost the same routine. He threw frozen chips in the oven, had a quick shower and then emerged to fry steak and toss a bit of salad. It was an unexciting diet but it kept him alive.

Nell wasn't complaining. Wrapped in her voluminous crimson bathrobe, she walked into the kitchen and wrinkled her nose in appreciation.

'Yum. No one told me you could cook.'

'It's hardly gourmet cooking.' He looked up from his frying-pan and found her eyes doing a careful assessment of him—from the toes up. The sensation was unnerving, to say the least. 'How…how do you like your steak?'

'Medium. So I'm sure it's dead.' She sniffed her appreciation. 'And chips, too. Wow! What a man!'

'You'll make me go all bashful,' he told her, grinning and trying desperately not to do just that. He was practically acting like a schoolboy! 'Sit down.' He went back to concentrating on his steak, but he was searingly aware of Nell's eyes following his every move.

'You can have some wine if you like,' she told him. 'I've slept all afternoon, and it's my turn to be on call, so you can eat and drink all you like and then fall into bed.'

Wonderful thought. Ridiculous thought!

'I need to go back to the hospital. I haven't done my rounds yet.'

'I can do those for you.'

'They're my responsibility.'

'You're sharing responsibility, remember?' She smiled up at him as he placed a loaded plate in front of her, and her smile made his guts move sideways. 'With me. And you've worked all afternoon while I've slept.'

'You're not doing my ward rounds.'

She glared. 'I'll sulk.'

'Sulk away.'

'I'll ring up Jonas and tell him you're not co-operating.'

'Fate worse than death. I can cope.'

'I'll strip naked!'

Blake's eyes flew wide at that, and she chortled. 'Got you there. That is a fate worse than death.' She looked down at her very pregnant bulge. 'And maybe you're right to back away in horror. Sexy I ain't.'

Sexy she most certainly was, with her gorgeous crimson robe and her tousled curls and her wide green eyes, but he wasn't saying that for the world.

'So tell me about your wife,' she said conversationally, ignoring his astonishment and popping a chip into her mouth. 'What was she like?'

That was enough to kill any vestige of amusement. 'You don't want to know about my wife.'

'Of course I want to know about your wife.' Another chip went the way of its predecessor and she twinkled. 'I'm the world's biggest sticky beak—that's me—and Jonas and Em told me just enough to be tantalising.'

'Well, get untantalised. I'm not talking.'

'Why not?'

He ate half his steak before answering, but his silence didn't work. Instead of being abashed, she was eyeing him like an inquisitive sparrow, and her probing laughter was almost impossible to resist. She ate and watched him, and he had the feeling she was laughing inside at his reticence. Finally he laid down his knife and fork and glared.

'You tell me first.'

'Tell you what?'

'I assume there's been a man in your life.' He was goaded into asking this. He didn't want to know, he told himself, but it might shut her up. And…he wouldn't mind knowing.

'You mean the father of my baby?'

'That'd be the one.' He lifted his fork again and pierced another slice of steak. Trying to pretend it didn't matter.

'You don't want to know about him. It's boring.'

'Then you don't want to know about my wife.'

She tilted her chin and regarded him across the table—considering. 'If I tell you mine, will you tell me yours?'

'We'd bore each other stupid.'

'But Emily says you've locked away what's happened and won't talk about it and it's driving you crazy.'

He grimaced at that. 'Em should mind her own business.'

'Em's a wonderful doctor. She cares.'

'She sticks her nose in—'

'Where it's not wanted. That's what good doctors do. You know as well as I do that the worst problems present as a grazed knee or a request for hayfever tablets, and then, if you leave a chink of silence at the end there's an ''Oh, by the way, Doctor…'' and out it all comes. Something really major, like they're feeling suicidal or they have a lump in their groin. And if you don't leave that chink, there's trouble.'

'But I don't need—'

'You do need.' Nell's smile faded and the look she directed at Blake was searching and concerned. 'Em's right. You've locked everything up and it's doing damage.'

'Don't be ridiculous.'

'So just tell me.'

'You tell me,' he said, goaded. 'If you have your life so under control…'

'I don't have my life under control.'

'Tell me about your baby's father.'

She took a deep breath. 'And you agree to tell me about your wife?'

He sighed, pushed to the limit. 'If I tell you, will you get off my back?'

'Never another word,' she said virtuously. 'Cross my heart and hope to break a leg.'

'Then tell me about yourself first,' he muttered, and tried to think back to how this conversation had ever got started. He should draw back right now. But she was sitting across the table from him, eating chip after chip, and her eyes were smiling and kind.

Damn it, he did want to know about her, and if the price was simply telling her about Sylvia...

He could wear it, he thought. Maybe.

'Who's the baby's father?' he growled. And waited.

To his surprise, her response took a long time coming. Nell finished her meal, pushed her plate away and sat looking down at the table for a long, long time.

She was as reluctant as he was, Blake thought, and the knowledge surprised him. Sylvia...well, Sylvia was a tragedy, but surely there was no tragedy with Nell. An indiscretion, maybe, but...

'I thought my baby's father was my husband.' Her soft voice cut across his thoughts and his eyes flew to hers.

'What?'

'Silly, wasn't I?' She gave a self-deprecating grin, but her laughter was completely gone. It was a forced grin. A smile of humiliation.

'Will you explain?'

'Maybe I need to go back...to go back further.'

'I have time.' He glanced at his watch. There was half an hour before he'd told the nursing staff he'd be back, and if she took all that time then maybe he wouldn't have to talk about Sylvia.

'Richard was the son of my grandfather's accountant.'

'I see.' But Blake didn't. 'Your grandfather was the local doctor here.'

'That's right.' She took a deep breath. 'He certainly was. But he hated me. As did my grandmother.'

'Surely not.'

'Of course they did. Ask anyone. My mother was their only child. She was brought up in a house of repression and dislike, and she got herself into trouble. With me. Then she disappeared, leaving my grandparents with what they termed the consequence of sin. It was their Christian duty to rear me but no one ever said they had to like it. They couldn't look their neighbours in the eye while I was around, and I couldn't leave.'

'Hell,' Blake said faintly, and Nell nodded.

'It was hell. My mother left when she was fifteen, and I should have left then, too. But somehow…' She sighed and looked up, meeting Blake's eyes over the table. 'I was good at school,' she told him. 'The teachers were kind, and I guess in some strange way I thought that maybe if I became a doctor—someone of worth like my grandfather—then I'd gain my grandparents' approval. I might have known it could never happen.'

He nodded. 'And so?'

Nell shrugged. 'So I worked my butt off, I won a scholarship to university, became a doctor and once I'd left, I never came home. Until my grandmother died.'

'Which was?'

'Two years back.'

'That's right.' His brow cleared. 'I'd just arrived in town. She was the old lady out on Beacon Point.'

'That's the one. My grandfather had died some years before and I contacted her then—while I was still at university. But she told me not to come home for the funeral because my grandfather wouldn't have wanted me there. So I didn't. But I came home to bury my grandmother. She had no one else.'

'And…'

'And I met Richard.' She sighed. 'He was with his father when they told me I'd inherited everything from my grandparents' estate.'

'So your grandparents were fond of you after all.'

'No way.' She shook her head. 'To leave me money would have been unthinkable. Heavens, I might have spent it! But they were so old-fashioned that Gran never thought about making a will in her own right. Grandpa left everything to her, and if she predeceased him then he left it all to charity. I guess he figured that'd cut me right out. But he was too private and too proud to use a lawyer, so he omitted planning for what eventually happened. Gran outlived him. She therefore inherited the lot and failed to make a will in her own right. Which left me with everything. By default.'

'Lucky you.'

'Maybe I was.' She gave a rueful smile. 'I didn't know how lucky. But Richard did. His father told him. They were misers, my grandparents, and I was suddenly worth a fortune. Do you see the irony in that? Poor, downtrodden Nell who everyone was told was worthless was suddenly almost a millionaire. Until then all I'd known was hard work. And then—my grandparents were gone and there was Richard.'

Richard... Blake thought back to vague gossip he'd heard just after he'd arrived in Sandy Ridge. And then more recently. The gossip hadn't been pleasant. 'Richard Lyons?'

'That's the one.'

'I see.' He did, too. Hell! 'And you fell for him?'

'Richard would have charmed blood from a stone,' she said bitterly. 'And I was so stupid I married him.' She shrugged. 'You have no idea what it was like... I'd been so damned alone, and my grandparents' deaths made me feel appalling. Richard was the wrong man at the wrong time. So I was a fool. He'd come here to spend time with his father—in fact, he'd come to ask for money but I didn't know that. He was desperate and I was the answer to his prayers.'

'And you married?'

'We married. Fast. Why wait? he said, and it made sense. I'd been alone too long, and he was so…loving.' She hugged herself and a shiver ran right through her. Suddenly Blake felt an almost overwhelming need to reach out and touch her—comfort her—but she kept speaking, and somehow he held back.

'Richard had a dubious accountancy practice back in Sydney,' she told him. 'It was near Sydney Central, so he moved into my flat and I kept on with my medicine. But the marriage wasn't happy. It didn't take me long to realise what an idiot I'd been. And then, just as I was thinking I should walk away, I became pregnant.'

'And…'

'And Richard demanded I have a termination. I wouldn't—I was so upset—and I caught the flu and I was morning sick and miserable. I was on night duty and my boss sent me home.' She shrugged. 'So I came home unexpectedly and it was the old story. I found Richard in bed with someone else.'

'I…see.' It was an inane comment but the best he could come up with.

'You don't see at all,' she said bitterly. 'You don't know how close I came to throwing it all in. And I mean everything. Suicide had never looked so good. But then I started walking—and walking the streets of Sydney at night when you're alone is not a good idea. It ended with me being mugged. And finding Ernest. Somehow we pulled ourselves together, we drove back here out to my grandparents' house and sat on the bluff and looked out to sea—for hours. And then I made a few decisions.'

'Which were?'

'To take control,' she said, and her chin jutted in a way he was coming to know. And like. 'To stop trying to please everyone and subjugating myself for scraps of affection.' She took a deep breath and she met Blake's gaze head on. 'I had a new little life aboard and I don't want my baby to have a doormat for a mother. And I had the world's best dog to take care of. So I headed to the best lawyer I could find. Nick Daniels at Bay Beach. He's a county court judge now but as a lawyer he's the best.'

'He helped you?'

'He certainly did.' Nell smiled. 'I had one piece of luck. I'd walked into the flat and heard Richard and his woman in bed, and I'd walked straight out again without them knowing I'd seen, so Richard still thought I was the adoring stupid little woman. He didn't have a clue I was onto him. And I was just in time. I rang Richard and told him I'd been called urgently to Bay Beach because a friend was ill. Then Nick and I started asking questions. I discovered so much of mine had been shifted to both our names—ready for Richard to remove everything. Nick was appalled. Apparently Richard had had it organised for months. But I forestalled him, and I won. For the first time in my life I won.'

'Good for you.'

'It was, wasn't it?' Laughter sprang back. 'Then I went back to Sydney, kicked Richard out of my flat and I got the king-sized quilt I'd been making. You have no idea how stupid I felt. I'd spent hours and hours making a stupid quilt for a marriage that was nothing but a fraud—and I chopped it up and made it into maternity overalls. And then I made a few more decisions. One of them was that I wanted to work here.'

Blake thought that through. 'Richard disappeared?'

'He and his lady had been planning to leave for a while,' Nell said bitterly. 'So, yes, they scampered—with lots of clients' money but, thanks to Nick, not mine.' She shrugged. 'He hurt a lot of people.'

'Including you.'

'No.' She shook her head. 'He didn't hurt me. He woke me up out of my stupor. He made me realise just how damned stupid I'd been and for how long. So I'm almost grateful.'

'Yeah?'

'Yeah.' She chuckled. 'Except if I saw him again I'd personally castrate the toerag. In the nicest possible way, of course.'

He raised his eyebrows at that. 'Oh, of course.'

'And the best thing was, when the police dug really deeply into his background they discovered he'd married before. About ten years ago. Even though it only lasted a few months he'd never bothered to get a divorce, so I wasn't married after all and I wasn't in any way responsible for all the debts he'd run up.' She took a deep breath. 'So now you know,' she told him. 'That's all. Now, are you going to tell me about you?'

'Me?'

'Yep, you, stupid. And your wife. Sylvia.'

'I…'

'Fair's fair and a bargain's a bargain.'

But then the phone rang. Saved by the bell, Blake thought thankfully, but Nell beat him to the receiver.

'Dr McKenzie here.' Then she listened. 'Right,' she said at last, her eyes on Blake's face. 'We'll be there in three minutes.'

She replaced the receiver. 'This doesn't let you off the hook,' she told him.

'No. But what is it?'

She was already moving toward the door. 'Grace Mayne's on her way in. Her neighbour found her. She's unconscious and the ambulance boys thinks she's dying.'

Hell! Grace…

'I'll go,' Blake snapped, reaching the door at the same time she did.

'Grace saved my life this morning,' Nell told him, her voice shaken yet determined. 'And Aaron's. We'll *both* go.' She hesitated. 'And then we'll come straight back here and take up where we left off.'

The ambulance boys had had a long day today. For minimally trained volunteers it was almost too much. Professional detachment wasn't in their job description. Bob and Henry stood by the stretcher and almost wrung their hands. They might enjoy a bit of drama, but not when it was as serious as it had been today.

'What happened?' Blake demanded answers before he reached Grace's side. He was moving so fast Nell almost had to trot to keep up with him. The fact that she was wearing her grandpa's overlong bathrobe didn't help at all.

But she was determined to keep up. Blake was determined to practise alone, and the only way to break him of the habit was to stick by him. Like glue.

And this was Grace... Oh, no. Grace! No wonder Bob and Henry looked sick. The old lady had held a place in the town's collective hearts since Nell had first met her. Whenever there'd been trouble, there'd been Grace. Whenever anyone had needed help, she'd been there. She had a heart so big...

Her heart. Please, let it not be her heart, Nell thought. If this morning's exertions were to kill her... Dear God, no!

But Grace looked dreadful. Blake already had his stethoscope out and his fingers were on the old lady's wrist, feeling her pulse as soon as he reached her. 'Does anyone know what happened?' he demanded again, and the ambulancemen nodded.

'Her neighbour, Adam Roberts,' Henry whispered, dragging his eyes from Grace's chest. It was hardly moving. She was hardly breathing. 'Adam was on the boat this morning, too.'

'And?' Blake's voice was clipped and decisive, dragging professionalism from him, and with an effort Henry made himself concentrate.

'Adam said they drove home together as soon as the boat moored,' he told them. Both ambulancemen were totally focussed on Grace. They hadn't spared Nell's startling outfit a glance. In fact, Nell had now shifted from being just another local. They no longer saw her as Nell. They saw her now as another doctor—more help—and the bathrobe didn't register at all.

'She was fine,' Bob continued. 'Adam said she ate a huge lunch—latish like. They cracked a bottle of champagne and Grace had three glasses. And then she felt a bit wobbly so she went for a lie-down. Adam was a bit concerned, so he popped in after dinner. He found her...' His voice broke off in distress.

Blake lifted the wrinkled eyelids. Grace's pupils were dilated and unresponsive. Nothing.

'Is it her heart?' Bob whispered, his face almost as ashen as Grace's. 'Hell...Grace... We thought Grace'd live for ever.'

So had everyone, Nell thought, feeling sick. She'd asked the old lady to take her out to sea. She'd done this to her!

'Had she taken her diabetic tablets?' Blake demanded across their grim thoughts, and Bob frowned.

'Diabetic tablets?'

But Henry knew. 'Yeah, she did,' he volunteered. 'Adam said to tell you that. He said they were late having lunch and with the champagne and everything she thought she should take two.'

'Two,' Blake said, his face clearing like magic. 'Nell, would you—?'

But Nell was already scrambling for the blood-sugar monitor. She handed it to Blake, and her heart was lifting. Two... Thank you, God. Oh, thank you. Wordlessly Blake took a pin-prick of blood. Seconds later he had the answer—and it was great!

'She's having a hypo,' he told them, unable to conceal his delight, already finding a vein. 'Her blood sugar's way down. It's almost zero.'

'You're kidding.' Bob and Henry had enough medical training to realise what that meant. 'Hell,' Henry said, staring down at Grace's limp form. 'You mean if we'd just given her juice... But...' His face clouded again. 'We couldn't. She was unconscious. Doc, she looks…she looks almost dead. Is it too late?'

'She's not and it certainly isn't,' Blake said firmly. 'Though she's obviously past a cure by a glass of juice. But I'm betting if we give her an injection of glucose she'll be back to normal in no time. Watch.'

And that was the way it was. Almost at the prick of the needle, Grace stirred and woke. It was one of medicine's nicest miracle cures, Nell thought, almost delirious with relief. Not a heart attack. Only a hypo. She closed her eyes and sat down in a nearby chair, her professional detachment flying straight out the window. Oh, Grace…

'I… Where…?' It was a faint whisper, echoing gloriously through the examination cubicle. The old lady was confused and upset, but she was already coherent, and Blake took her hand and held it. Hard.

'You've had a diabetic hypo,' he told her, his voice gentle but steady. 'You remember? It's the thing I'm always warning you against. Taking two tablets indeed…'

Grace's eyes creased in confusion, but Blake's eyes were sure and reassuring. Finally she searched the room and her eyes found Nell. 'It's Nell,' she said, her voice wondering.

Nell thought, She recognises me. All this and she still recognises me. But she hardly knows me. 'You scared the life out of us,' she managed. 'Oh, Grace…'

'I never meant to. Oh, girl, I'm so sorry.'

'Don't you be sorry.' Nell found her feet and found her smile and stooped to hug Grace. 'Don't you dare be sorry. After all you've done today… You deserve to do whatever you want.'

'Except kill yourself with neglect,' Blake growled, trying to keep his own emotions under control. 'OK, Grace. We'll organise you a meal. We'll keep your blood sugar monitored all night and you're not going home until it's steady.' He shook his head. 'I've had enough trouble with the fishing community for one day.'

Grace was recovered enough to grin. 'No. How can you

say that? You just got to sit on a ledge while we risked life and limb.'

'Yeah? A ledge made of crumbling sandstone…'

'It's the women who're the toughest,' Grace said serenely, and for some reason her old eyes rested on Nell's with something that looked astonishingly like affection. And caring.

'Says who?' Blake's relief at the outcome was making him feel fantastic. With Nell safe by his side…

Now why had he thought that?

'Let's get you into the ward,' he growled, and he found all of them were looking at him in astonishment.

'Do you need to sound grumpy?' Grace shook her head. 'And I'm not staying here. Bob, take me home.'

'Bob, wheel her into the ward.' Blake had himself together again—almost. He lifted his syringe. 'You need a meal and then a sleep, with us monitoring your blood sugar at regular intervals, and you're not going home until I'm convinced you're settled.' He held the sharp needle against the light, and then looked at Grace, considering. 'So…do you want to go quietly, or do you want to suffer the consequences?'

And Grace laughed and held up her hands in mock surrender. 'OK, Dr Sutherland,' she conceded. 'You're the boss.'

'That's just the way I like it,' Blake said, and Nell grinned. She did like a happy ending. Especially this one.

'It's time you went home to bed, too,' Blake told her. 'I'll stay and do my ward rounds.'

'I'll do them with you.'

'There's no need.'

'You know damned well there's a need,' she said severely. 'Grace, this man's avoiding me. What do you make of that?'

'I think any man who avoids a girl in nightwear as gorgeous as yours needs his head read,' Grace said stoutly, recovering by the minute.

Her nightwear… 'Oh, help.' Then Nell grinned and did a pirouette right there and then. God was in his heaven, and all was right with Nell's world.

Grace smiled, and this time there was no mistaking her affection. 'It makes a change from a white coat,' she told her.

There was that. 'It does indeed,' Nell agreed. And then, before he could guess what she intended, Nell tucked her hand in Blake's. 'Come on, Dr, Sutherland. Let's get on with it.' She smiled at Bob and Henry, and then at Grace, encompassing them all in her happiness. 'Dr Sutherland and I are going to do his ward rounds and then he's going to tell me his life story. What do you think of that?'

Grace smiled. 'I think Dr Sutherland had better be careful.' She hesitated. 'Looks like the days of a lone medico are over. By the look of the pair of you, in thirty years Nell could be as entangled in the concerns of this town as I am.' And her smile said she thought that was no bad fate at all.

Not like Blake. His hand in Nell's was suddenly rigid. 'I don't think so.'

'Don't fight against the tide,' Grace told him, still smiling. 'There's nought you can do about it—and would you really want to try?'

Yes!

But for now he had no choice. Nell's hand lay in his, she was waiting and he had no choice but to get on with it. It was either that or pick her up bodily and put her out of the door. That was maybe an appealing option, he thought grimly, but she was smiling at him, too.

Fight against the tide? Some things were just impossible.

CHAPTER SEVEN

IT WAS over an hour later before Nell had Blake where she wanted him—back in the kitchen with a pot of coffee between them. 'Now,' she said severely, and he shook his head.

'Now I need to finish my coffee and go to bed. I'd imagine you do, too.'

'I'm not going anywhere. I slept all afternoon and I'm not tired, so stop prevaricating. It's your turn to talk, Dr Sutherland. I told you the "How Nell Was a Dope" story with all the gory details. Now you tell me "Why Blake Swore Off Relationships For Ever". I'm listening.'

He didn't want to. He drank his coffee too fast and then rose from the table. Nell's hand reached out and caught his, pulling him back.

'No,' she said severely. 'Sit.'

He managed a smile at that. 'Hey, I'm not Ernest.'

'No. But sit, all the same.' She didn't release his hand, and he stared down at their intertwined fingers. Her hand felt warm and strong. Despite his wish to stay uninvolved with this amazing woman, the story she'd told him flooded back.

What sort of people had her grandparents been? he wondered. He remembered the old lady—fiercely independent and almost paranoid with pride. It had taken every inch of his skill to persuade her to allow nurses into her home for those last few months. He hadn't warmed to her at all.

And now… Letting his hand rest in Nell's, he felt an almost overwhelming longing for the old lady to still be alive. So he could go and shout at her—ask her what the hell she thought she'd been doing to allow Nell to have that sort of dreadful, barren childhood.

If she'd been adopted she'd have been loved to bits, he thought. Anyone would love her. She deserved to be loved.

If she'd been loved in childhood she wouldn't be in this mess, he thought bitterly, and then the thought came out of left field.

He wouldn't be in this mess!

'Hey, it's not that bad,' she murmured, and his eyes flew to hers.

'What?'

'You look angry. Does sharing your past make you cross?'

'No, I...'

'You are going to tell me—aren't you?'

Blake took a deep breath. 'There's nothing to tell. I was married and now I'm not. Sylvia's dead.'

'I know that. Em said your wife was killed in a car crash.'

'That's right. End of story. So what else do you want to know?'

'Why Em says the mention of her name makes you clam up. Why you can't talk about her. Why it still hurts so damned much.'

'She was killed.'

'Yes, but that doesn't explain it,' she said as if he was being deliberately obtuse. 'After three years she should be fading to a beloved memory. She shouldn't be stabbing you with pain. Stopping you living to the full.'

'You don't understand.'

'So explain. Make me understand.'

He glared. 'You need to be in bed.'

And she glared back. Desperate measures were called for. How had she made him do what she wanted in the past? Yeah, right.

Nell grinned and felt for the top button of her bathrobe. 'Blake Sutherland, you have two minutes,' she said, exasperated. 'And then I'm starting to strip.' She undid her top button, her eyes daring him. 'One button at a time. All the way.'

Good grief! He eyed her uneasily. Make a joke, he told himself desperately. Hell, how else could he cope? 'Is this the line you try on patients who are reluctant to tell you their problems?'

'All the time,' she said serenely, and he almost choked.

'I don't believe you.'

Her fingers moved to the next button. 'Try me.'

'I'll head back to the hospital.'

'I'll follow you to the hospital,' she said. 'Stark naked.'

'You wouldn't dare.'

'No?' Her green eyes sparked with mischief, and she undid the next button. 'Are you sure?'

And then she undid the next...

Blake didn't depend in the least on her good sense—or her sense of decency, he decided. Her good sense should have prevented her trying to go out through the harbour mouth this morning, and she'd risked drowning instead. Compared to that, a naked display in the grounds of the hospital would be nothing.

Despite himself, his lips twitched. She saw, and she smiled encouragingly.

'You should know I don't threaten what I can't deliver. So tell me.'

'You're incorrigible.'

She chuckled. 'That's the nicest thing anyone's ever said about me. Incorrigible. I like it.'

'Nell...'

'Just tell me.'

He sighed. He sighed again but her look was stern.

'Come on.'

And there was no choice. Tentatively he tried, but it hurt. It hurt even to say the name. 'Sylvia...'

Nell sighed, exasperated. 'Your wife's name was Sylvia. I know that. What else?'

'She was a mistake.'

'Well, join the club,' Nell said without rancour. 'You and Sylvia. Me and Richard. I bet Richard was the biggest disaster, though.'

'Not necessarily. In fact, not even remotely.'

He still seemed reluctant to continue so Nell prodded some more. 'So let me guess. She was a nymphomaniac who insisted on sleeping naked?'

He couldn't help it. His mouth twisted into a smile, and Nell smiled with him. 'That's better,' she approved. 'Tell me more.'

'I...'

'Oh, for heaven's sake, just do it,' she snapped, losing patience. 'Now.'

And he cast her one last long look—and started to talk.

'Sylvia was another doctor,' he said, and his tone was different now. Dispassionate. It was as if what he was talking about concerned someone else—not him. 'We met in final year—at a hospital Christmas celebration. She was gorgeous, intelligent, funny... In fact, she was everything I thought I wanted in a wife.'

'I see.' There was a tiny bit of Nell that didn't like this, but surely it was illogical. What he thought of his dead wife had nothing to do with her—did it?

'I'd been a swot,' he told her, his voice still expressionless. 'Like you, I was a scholarship kid. If I didn't do well, I lost my funding, so I'd been head down, butt up in my books for years. It was Christmas. I'd just passed my final exams, I raised my head from my books and almost had it knocked off by Sylvia.'

'You fell for her?'

'Hook, line and sinker.' He shrugged, and smiled a smile that didn't reach his eyes. 'So much so that I asked her to marry me.'

'And she did?'

'No.' He shook his head, and his gaze fell to the wedding ring on his finger. 'Not then.'

'Why not?'

'Sylvia was having too much fun. She was so smart…' He shook his head again. 'She'd hardly had to study. Exams were something the rest of us fretted about, but not Sylvia. If she couldn't get away with her extraordinary intelligence she charmed her way through them. And she seemed to hardly need sleep.'

He shrugged. 'Anyway, as soon as the Christmas break was over and we settled back to work I could see the whole affair was stupid. Doomed. I wanted to do my surgical training so I needed to sleep and to study, and she didn't. She thought I was boring. So… We graduated, I took up surgery and she took off for Europe. I expected never to see her again.'

'Poor dear.' Nell smiled with mock sympathy. She could imagine Blake as a recently graduated doctor, and she could also envisage what life must have been like for him then. Medical students might be too busy for a love life, but absurdly good-looking fully qualified young doctors as Blake must have been most definitely were not. 'I can't actually see you broken-hearted and bereft.'

He glanced up at that and met her dancing eyes, and he managed a grin himself.

'Well, no. Not really.'

She chuckled. 'You hardly have the look of a man who'd go unnoticed by the female population in general. After leaving the rigours of medical school behind you, I bet you went from girl to girl.'

'Hardly that. But…' His grin faded. 'OK, I had a good time, but I never felt settled. Even when I finished my surgical training, it was like Sylvia had left a shadow—a ghost I couldn't exorcise. After a while I left Sydney and took up a consultant's post at Niribil in Western Australia. Niribil's about the size of Blairglen. I did general surgery rather than vascular surgery but I enjoyed the country. I enjoyed a smaller, familiar practice where everyone knew everyone.' He took a deep breath. 'And then Sylvia came home.'

'I see.'

'I bet you don't.' His voice was suddenly savage. 'She was different. More fragile somehow. Brittle. But still breathtakingly lovely. She was on my doorstep when I got home from hospital one night, and she said simply that she'd missed me dreadfully and if I still wanted to, we'd be married. Straight away.'

'So you were?'

'Well, what would you have done?' Blake closed his eyes in remembered pain. 'Hell, I'd asked her more than once. I'd said if ever she changed her mind I was still there for her. And she was still lovely.'

'But?'

'Yeah, there's a but,' he said grimly. 'Of course. I should have waited. It had been years since we'd been together, and we needed time. She didn't give us time, and when I discovered what was wrong we were well and truly married. She was up to her neck in substance abuse.'

'Oh, no…'

'She'd thought she was so clever,' he said grimly. 'Apparently it had started before she finished medical school. Uppers to get her through the exams, tranquillisers to get her to sleep and then a frightening progression to the heavy stuff. When we'd thought she was just naturally bouncy she was really as high as a kite. Much of this, though, I didn't find out until later.'

'How much later?'

'After she was dead.'

Nell drew in her breath. 'Oh, Blake…' Then she went on gently, 'Do you want to tell me? I won't insist.'

There was a moment's pause. And then he shrugged. 'Why not? Why not tell you everything? I've come this far.' He took a deep breath. 'As soon as she arrived, Sylvia applied for a registrar's job at Niribil. There was no hesitation in employing her. After all, I knew her qualifications

were sound. In view of the fact that I vouched for her—
and that I was marrying her—the hospital board didn't even
bother to check her employment record in Europe. If they
had…'

'If they had?'

'Then they'd have found out she had two malpractice
suits coming up against her. Major ones. For gross negli-
gence. Which was why she'd fled back to Australia.' He
chewed his bottom lip. 'Anyway…'

'Anyway?'

'Anyway, we married,' he said grimly. 'And I started
worrying almost straight away. You can't live with someone for long without suspecting things aren't OK. But I
didn't know for sure, and I didn't say anything. After all,
how could I be so crass as to suggest my wife was a drug
addict?'

'It wasn't obvious?'

'It was obvious that she was either high or low. Almost
as soon as we were married I saw the mood swings that
she'd been careful to keep from me, and I suspected psy-
chological problems. But before I could do anything about
it a little boy came into Casualty with meningitis. Sylvia
had been employed as the emergency registrar, but she'd
gone home early, leaving no doctor on duty. The nursing
staff saw him and were worried, suspecting meningitis. So
they rang Sylvia. But Sylvia couldn't be bothered to get
out of bed. She gave phone orders for a dose of antibiotics
that was a tenth of what was needed, and said she'd see
him in the morning.'

'Oh, no… Oh, Blake…'

'When the child's condition worsened they tried again,'
he went on inexorably. 'But they couldn't raise Sylvia any
more. And no wonder. She was zonked out of her brain—
almost unconscious.'

'Where were you?'

'I was up to my neck in Theatre, dealing with a car-
accident emergency. When the little boy started deteriorat-

ing the charge nurse came to find me to ask how they could raise Sylvia, but by that time the kid had been in trouble for six hours. And he'd lapsed into a coma. I changed the antibiotic orders—any fool would have and the charge nurse should have seen it himself. When I finished operating I took over Sylvia's role, but it was far, far too late. And when the little boy died, I went to find her.'

It made everything so clear. Dreadful but clear. 'And…'

'And I couldn't wake her. So I went through her bedside cabinet. Six weeks married.' He gave a harsh laugh. 'I couldn't believe what I found. I couldn't believe I'd been so stupid. She'd taken so much…'

He closed his eyes on remembered pain. 'I was so furious. Unbelievably—explosively angry. And then, when she finally woke and I told her what had happened, she turned into the Sylvia who'd laughed when I'd first proposed marriage. Supercilious. She said I was being ridiculous, and she didn't have to put up with this. Before I could stop her she'd headed out to the car and driven off. Fast. Too damned fast. I sent the police after her and went searching myself, but she went over the cliff a couple of miles out of town.'

'Oh, Blake…'

'Pathetic, wasn't it?' He gave a ghost of a dreadful smile. 'The town had employed her because of me, and I was too stupid to see what was happening. I failed them.' He looked down at his hand, and he twisted the ring. 'And I failed Sylvia.'

'How do you figure that?'

'I should have seen. Maybe I did, but I didn't want to know. I was so damned busy. I was too damned smitten.' He took the ring from his finger and then replaced it, like it was a chain that held him a prisoner. 'Anyway, I moved. I came here. I decided I'd practise alone. I wouldn't depend on anyone.' He raised his head and met Nell's look head on. 'And I don't.'

She hesitated. 'But you need me.'

'I don't need you,' he said flatly. 'I don't need anyone.'

'You're running yourself into the ground.'

'No.'

Her hand came across the table again and took his. She held it firmly, using both of her hands to hold his one, and her eyes were direct and deadly serious.

'Blake, you can't stay alone for ever because of one stupid mistake.'

'Tommy Vanderboort will be dead for ever because of my mistake. He was six years old and he's dead. And so is Sylvia.'

'So one day we'll all be dead,' she said, exasperated. 'But, meanwhile, you need to get a life.'

'I have a life.'

'Yeah, medicine, which can very easily be shared. That's why I'm here.'

'For four weeks.'

'I'm here for ever,' she said bluntly. 'And I want to work. You may as well use me.'

But Blake's mind had closed against her. The remembered pain was still reflected in his eyes. 'I'll use you over the Christmas rush,' he told her. 'Until you need to go to Blairglen to have your baby. But that's all. I won't depend on anyone else.'

'So you'll take the medical needs of the whole community on your shoulders alone—for how long? Until you collapse of a nervous breakdown?'

'Don't be ridiculous.'

'It's you who's ridiculous,' she snapped.

'Look, let's leave it.'

'No.'

His face shuttered in anger. 'Leave it, Dr McKenzie. You're employed for four weeks. No longer. The board won't put you on permanently without my approval.'

'And you won't give it?'

'That's right.'

'Then you're a fool.'

'Thanks very much.'

'Think nothing of it.' And then her mood suddenly seemed to lighten and she smiled. It was an extraordinary smile, given the circumstances. 'Hmm.' She pushed herself back in the chair and surveyed him thoughtfully. 'Look, this is crazy. You and me…we're a right pair. We've both had marital disasters. The only difference is that I refuse to let it wreck my life—in fact, I figure it might well have been the catalyst for me to start living. You've decided otherwise. So I only have three weeks left to change your mind.'

'I won't change my mind.'

'I'm not a drug addict.'

'No, but you're a…'

'A woman?'

'Yes!'

'Well, how about that?' she said slowly, and her smile widened. 'Well, well. So, if I had a sex-change operation, it'd be OK to employ me?'

'No, but…'

'But what?'

'Nothing.' Blake shoved himself back from the table so hard the chair fell over. 'Nothing at all. I'm going back to the hospital.' He hesitated. 'There's some orders for Aaron I forgot to write up.'

She didn't believe him, and it showed, but she was being polite. 'You do that, Dr Sutherland,' she told him cordially, and her smile didn't slip. 'Off you go. Minister to the sick and needy all by yourself.'

'I—'

'Don't let me stop you.' What the hell was she playing at? She was still laughing. 'What a hero. But if you're setting yourself up as a hero, then I'll be a heroine.'

'What do you mean by that?'

'Meaning that if you can be a drama king then I can be a queen to match,' she said kindly. 'I made a fool of myself over a man, and you did the same over a woman. But I

took off my wedding ring and threw it into the middle of
next week. You should do the same.'

'No.'

'You will.'

'Nell…'

But she appeared to be thinking and her attention didn't
seem to be on him. 'Three weeks. It's not very long.'

'I can't—'

'But Christmas is in between.' She wrinkled her forehead, deep in thought. 'All that brandy sauce. It might do
the trick.'

'Nell!'

'Now, don't you worry about a thing.' Her smile deepened. 'Leave it to me.'

'Leave what to you?'

'Curing your broken heart, of course,' she said. 'After
all, I'm an expert. I chopped up my king-sized quilt and it
fixed me. What can we chop up of yours?'

'Nothing.'

'I'll think of something.' Her brow creased even more.
Then she looked up at him and smiled. 'What are you wait-
ing for? You have work to do and I have thinking to do.
So let's start now.' She waved him away and she smiled.
'Go on, then. Shoo!'

'But—'

'But nothing,' she told him. 'Just go! Leave Ernest and
me to our thinking.'

He'd never been told to shoo in his life before. But he
had no choice. Blake Sutherland…shooed.

It was a tricky problem.

Nell sat underneath the Christmas tree and threaded a bit
more popcorn and ate a lot more, and then she hugged
Ernest and fed him the rest. 'Because I'm getting as fat as
a whale,' she told him. 'If this bulge is all baby then I'm
having a twenty-pound whopper.'

Ernest looked at her with sympathy—and obligingly scoffed her popcorn.

'But what will we do with Blake?'

Ernest patently didn't know.

'So it's over to me.'

Ernest scoffed the last of the popcorn and looked hopefully toward the kitchen—just in case she was thinking of popping more. Which she wasn't.

'You're thinking it's none of my business?'

It was certainly none of Ernest's business. All he could focus on was popcorn.

'I certainly don't need the complications of hauling Blake Sutherland back to the real world.' Nell nodded and considered. 'But I do need a part-time job in medicine. I don't want to give up my medicine for ever, and I want to stay here.'

Hmm.

'You think I should leave all this until after this baby's born?' she demanded of Ernest. 'Let Blake stew in his own juice for a bit? Maybe that'd work. But Emily says he's headed for a breakdown and she's right.'

Ernest licked her hand, but Nell was oblivious. She scratched Ernest's ear, deep in thought. 'So should we let him break down, then leap into the breach and fix it? Like a true heroine? And a true heroine's dog?'

She gave a rueful grin to herself and ran a finger down the small of Ernest's back. Ernest almost turned inside out with pleasure.

But Nell was still thinking. 'That way I might lose him completely,' she said out loud. 'We all might. And the town doesn't want that.'

'Why not?' she demanded of herself.

'Because he's a wonderful doctor,' she retorted—but there was a part of her that knew she was lying. This wasn't anything to do with the fact that Blake was a wonderful doctor. And it had nothing to do with the medical needs of the town.

He was a very intriguing man. And maybe he was something more that she was hardly admitting to herself.

Yet…

CHAPTER EIGHT

FIVE a.m. Blake stirred from sleep and peered at his bedside clock. Something had woken him. Not the phone. What?

He threw back his covers and made his way out to the living room—and stopped short.

Nell was sitting beneath the Christmas tree. Ernest was snuggled in by her side and she was balancing a cup of tea on her very pregnant tummy.

She was wearing pyjamas covered with pink elephants. She looked cute and desirable and very, very alone. She looked like someone who he should just walk across to and gather into his arms and...

Hell! What on earth was he thinking of? He gave himself a mental shake and pushed the door wider. 'What are you doing?' he said carefully, and her cup of tea jumped on her bulge, splashing her pyjamas.

'Damn,' she said crossly. 'That's the third time I've sploshed.'

'The third time?'

'My bump actually doesn't make a very good table,' she admitted. 'Not when junior kicks. He's bumped it twice and now you've scared me into bumping it again.'

'I'm sorry.' He paused. 'What did you say you were doing?'

She smiled up at him, and his impression of cuteness and desirability and...and, despite the smile, forlornness deepened even further. 'I didn't,' she told him.

'Oh.' He paused. The situation was weirdly intimate. He was suddenly conscious of his own pyjamas—and the fact that he was wearing only the trousers. His chest felt very bare—and Nell was so damned close that...

Stop it!

What on earth was she doing? 'Are you going to tell me?' he demanded.

She considered. 'Would you believe I'm waiting for Santa Claus?'

He grinned. 'You'll have a long wait. There's still a week to go.'

'I'm a very patient woman.'

'You're a very pregnant woman,' he said gently. 'You should be in bed.'

She looked up at him then, surprised by the gentleness of his tone. Touched, even.

'Thanks, but you try telling that to Cornelius.'

'He's giving you trouble?'

'He's kicking his mother,' she said with dignity. 'You'd think he'd know better. Boy, will I have some words to say to him when he comes out.'

Blake hesitated. He should go back to bed. He should leave her there. But the temptation to do the opposite was suddenly impossible to resist.

He resisted no longer. He crossed the room and sat down beside her, and her look of surprise deepened.

'So what's your excuse?' she asked. 'Who's kicking you?'

'No one,' he admitted. 'But Ernest's thumping woke me up.' That's what it must have been, he decided. The goofy dog was in seventh heaven. His head was on Nell's knee and his tail was banging against the floor like a drumstick going flat out.

'Oh, heck.' Nell shoved a hand down and tried to still the offending thumping appendage. 'I'm sorry. I'll make him stop.'

Which was easier said than done. Her hand moved up and down with the tail. Ernest was as strong as a horse and his tail was determinedly cheerful.

Blake grinned. 'Right, then, Dr McKenzie. You'll make him stop. So how are you going to do that?'

'Most cocker spaniels have their tails chopped off at birth,' she said. And then she looked at the tail. Its thumping was an expression of pure bliss. 'Though how anyone could…' She sighed. 'I guess that's another way of saying I haven't a clue. I think as a disciplinarian I'm a failure.'

'You're not a failure.' Blake was sitting on the plush Turkish rug beside her. Above their heads were his three Christmas angels. They should have twinkly lights, he thought inconsequentially, and made a mental note to buy some, because suddenly it seemed important. Meanwhile, somehow he forced himself back to what Nell was saying.

'It's nice of you to say I'm not a failure, but so far I don't seem to have managed very well,' she told him. She took a deep breath. 'And how I'm going to manage being a mother…'

'You'll be a wonderful mother.'

She cast him an unsure glance. 'Do you think so? It scares me stupid.'

'Why wouldn't you be a good mother?' he demanded, and her look of uncertainty deepened.

'I have no role model. Except my grandparents. And they were great teachers—I don't think! If I follow their example, the very first time my baby annoys me I'll order her to leave home. I'll tell her she's useless and that she's only in the way.'

He grimaced. 'That's what you were told?'

'All the time.'

'Do you know what happened to your own mother?' he asked carefully. This wasn't a scene he would have chosen to share—it was too damned intimate for his liking—but leaving her alone now would have been selfish.

Selfish on whose part? Not his, he had to admit, because he wanted to stay.

'She's dead.'

'You're sure?'

'Mmm.' Nell nodded. 'I made enquiries almost as soon as I graduated and earned enough to pay an investigator.'

She shrugged. 'So I found out, but it doesn't make pretty telling. Fifteen-year-olds who are kicked out of home because they're pregnant rarely end up living happily ever after.'

He nodded wordlessly. As a doctor, he'd seen enough of the lives street kids led to know she was speaking the truth. 'Your grandparents have a lot to answer for.'

'They do at that.'

'But you're not in the least like them,' he told her, sure of that at least. 'And your mother and father must have been really special people to have produced you.'

'I don't even know who my father was.'

He looked at her sideways and thought this through. And smiled. 'I bet he had freckles.'

'Probably. And red hair because my mother was a blonde.' But she didn't smile. Her eyes had lost their customary laughter and the echoes of sadness were there in its place.

'You'd like to know your father?'

'I'd like to know anybody,' she said simply. 'My grandparents didn't want me. My mother's dead. I have no one.' She took a deep breath. 'Normally I don't mind but sometimes it's so damned lonely. I guess that's why I was stupid enough to fall for Richard.'

'You won't be alone for ever. There'll be someone else.'

'Oh, sure. I'm *so* desirable.' She managed a smile then, but it was a feeble one. 'Me and my baby and my best dog, Ernest.'

Blake wasn't to be deflected. 'Lots of men would think you were desirable.'

She fixed him with a look. 'Ha! You don't.'

'But I'm…'

'Different?' She tried to smile again but it didn't quite come off. 'I know. You've told me. Alone for life. Just like me. Only my aloneness isn't by choice.'

'It really worries you?'

'It's so damned hard,' she blurted out. 'Not the loneliness

bit. At least not for me. I can cope with that. But my baby...
Hell, my baby's father doesn't want her. He wanted me to
have a termination, and I'm betting he never comes near
me. In fact, even if he does surface he'll end up in jail, and
how useful's a jailbird as a father? If anything happened to
me, what would happen to my baby?'

He met her fear head on. 'Then it's lucky you're as
strong as a horse.'

'That sounds defensive.'

'It wasn't meant to sound defensive. It was meant to
sound reassuring. Pregnant women get odd fancies...'

'That they might die in childbirth.' She was glaring at
full strength now. 'Yeah. Really unrealistic. But you're a
doctor. You know it happens.'

'What happens?'

'Mothers die. If I got eclampsia...'

He was startled at that. Eclampsia... 'You're being
checked?'

'I'm checking myself.'

'You shouldn't be checking yourself.' He felt a surge of
real concern. Hell, if she did have eclampsia... 'Nell, for
heaven's sake. Are you OK?'

'Well, yes.' she admitted. 'I guess I am. Emily checked
me over last week and before that I saw the best obstetri-
cian Sydney Central has. But...'

Blake's breath was let out in a whoosh of relief. 'There
you go, then. What's your resting blood pressure?'

'Ninety over seventy.'

'That's great. Perfectly normal.'

'I know that.' She glared on, refusing to let go of her
terrors. 'But I still might get eclampsia. And I might die.'

'Is that why you're sitting out here, then?' he demanded,
things becoming clear. 'Worrying about dying?'

She hesitated. And, finally, she let go. 'A bit,' she admitted. 'I guess I've been worrying about who'll fill my
daughter's Christmas stocking next year if I do.'

'Or your son's?'

'As you say. Or my son's.'

He thought about this, trying to be professional—as he'd be if he were sitting on one side of his desk while his patient voiced her fears from the other. 'You really do have no one?'

'I really do have no one.' She took a deep breath, fighting to regain her normal cheerfulness. 'There's only Ernest and I can't see him changing nappies. Bay Beach has great children's homes, though.'

'You're so worried you checked out the orphanage?' he demanded, startled, and she gave a shamefaced nod.

'Just a bit.'

'Just a lot!' He could see it all now. Rationality had gone out the window. She'd been alone throughout this pregnancy and she'd lost perspective.

So she needed reassurance. Tell her she'll be fine, he told himself. Tell her there was less than a chance in a thousand that things would go wrong. Tell her...

But suddenly he knew what he'd tell her, and it was none of the above.

'I'll look after your baby if anything happens to you.'

He'd said it—and neither of them could believe he had. They sat on the floor and stared at each other and he thought, What on earth have I done?

And she thought, What on earth is he saying?

'Blake...'

'Nell?'

'You don't...you don't mean it?' she whispered, and the look on her face was one he was starting to know. And he didn't like it. It was her Nell-against-the-world look. Nell declaring she didn't need anyone.

It was Nell kick-starting her new life in her wonderful patchwork overalls and with a heartful of courage that was so much greater than any he had.

What he was offering was a tiny thing, he thought—a promise for an outcome he knew would never happen. But it meant the world to her. Her eyes were shining, shimmering with unshed tears, and her hand caught his and held.

'Blake, how could you? You don't have the least idea of what you're saying. You're a dyed-in-the-wool bachelor and the last thing you need is a baby.'

Yeah, but it'd be Nell's baby.

The thought hit home with quite amazing clarity that he wouldn't mind so much. If this baby was like Nell. A child... He could get a housekeeper, he thought. Bring it up here. Keep Ernest...

Hell, Nell wasn't going to die! But if she did...

It was a dreadful thought. Appalling. And he'd have a baby.

'Where would you squeeze a baby into your schedule?' she demanded, and he chuckled at the horror in her voice.

'So I guess you'd better live, then.'

'But...you are serious?'

Blake's laughter died. 'Yes, Nell. God knows why, but I am serious.'

'Even though you never want to marry again? You never want a woman? But you'd still take on a child.'

'If he or she needed me. Yes, I would.' And he knew, suddenly, that he spoke the truth.

'Oh, Blake...'

He gazed down at her upturned face, still trying to come to terms with what he'd offered. He must be mad. But he didn't feel in the least mad. He felt sure and strong, and warm and tender and...

And then, before he knew what she intended—before he could even guess—she'd twisted and taken his face between her two hands. And she'd kissed him full on the mouth.

The kiss was supposed to be one of gratitude—of surprise and pleasure and overwhelming thankfulness that he'd made such an offer—that he'd eased such an aching fear within.

But it never could be simple gratitude. Never. Because

the two of them had been apart for too long—partnerless— each of them aching with loneliness and with need. So there was that between them which neither understood but which became apparent at the first touch of lips to lips.

And it was something that was mind-shattering. It was like their world was blown apart at first touch.

Fire to fire…

That was what it was like, Nell thought dazedly. Wild- fire! She'd made the first move—she'd reached up to kiss Blake—but the moment they touched she was no longer in control. Her body had a life all of its own, and it was an all-engulfing blaze of white-hot heat.

Her mouth met his, and was it hers who claimed his or the other way around? Who knew? Nell didn't. All she knew was that there was warmth where there had only been ice before, and there was comfort and longing and aching, aching need…

He felt so good. He felt so right! From the first time she'd seen him she'd felt this magnetic pull between them, and it had grown stronger with every piece of evidence that here before her was a wonderful human being.

No. Not just a wonderful human being, she thought dazedly. A wonderful man.

He was big and tender and caring, and aching with the desolation of loss himself. He was as different to Richard as he could be.

He was…

He was Blake. Just Blake. And that was enough and more for her body to respond. She melted into him, aching to have his arms come around her and hold her. And when they did she could hardly believe it. Miracles did happen. Love could flower where there'd only been barren waste…

Love.

She was falling in love, she thought, bewildered beyond belief, and then she thought, No.

She wasn't falling. She'd fallen.

She was head over heels in love with Blake Sutherland,

she decided right there and then, and there wasn't a darn thing she could do to stop herself being just that.

And she wasn't going to begin to try.

And Blake… He had no idea what was going on. No idea at all. One minute he was sitting on the living-room floor under the ridiculously decorated Christmas tree, trying hard to be professional, trying hard to be concerned, and suddenly the axis of his world had tilted.

He hadn't meant to make such an offer. He hadn't meant to get involved at all. Hell, he never got involved. He was a doctor, for heaven's sake, and he heard hard-luck stories every day of the week. What if he offered every single mother the reassurance he'd just offered Nell?

But this wasn't any single mum. This was Nell.

It didn't make any sense at all, he told himself desperately, but the way his body was responding to hers, the way his head was threatening to explode and his thighs were on fire and his body was screaming his need and…

And hell!

If only he was wearing something on his upper body! But he was naked to the waist and her crazy pyjamas were brushing his bare skin, and her breasts were against his chest and…

And his arms came around and held her to him. It was a measure of reassurance, he told himself desperately. Not so he could deepen the kiss. Not so he could feel her gorgeous body against his. Both those things were side issues and they didn't matter.

Like hell they didn't matter! They were *all* that mattered. His mouth was plundering hers, starving for something he hardly knew he'd been missing. Or something that he'd never had.

Had he ever felt this way with Sylvia?

No. No and no and no.

Sylvia…

But suddenly she was there. His dead wife. She was in

his brain, screaming at him that letting his emotions rule his head led to disaster. Not just for him. For everybody.

A tiny six-year-old was dead because of his stupid emotions…

Once before he'd let his emotions hold sway and two people had died because of it. It was a desperate lesson, but it had been drilled in so far that even now it surfaced.

The way he was feeling was crazy. Terrible! The way Nell made him feel… Like it or not, he was emotionally involved, and this was the way of madness.

What was he doing? he thought dazedly. It was one thing to offer to care for a child when he knew that offer need never be taken up. It was another to kiss the child's mother as if he meant it.

He was falling toward… Falling toward he didn't know what, and it scared the life out of him. He didn't want this sort of involvement. *He didn't.*

And so, finally and with a shuddering gasp that left him feeling desolate with loss, he managed to pull away. Confused, Nell fell back, and she looked up at him in the dim light with eyes that were enormous. Her eyes reflected his confusion and his…his fear?

And that's what it was all about, he thought bitterly. Fear. Somehow he dragged himself to his feet, though afterwards he could never figure out how he'd done it. How he'd managed to break the link.

He was afraid, but at least he had the sense to admit it. To run before it could get any worse. 'I'm sorry. Nell, I'm sorry.' His voice was a husky whisper.

'Hey, I'm the one who kissed you.' She was striving for lightness but it didn't come off. How could it? 'I guess we've both been alone for two long. Sex-starved medicos, that's us.' And if her voice hadn't trembled he'd have thought she was joking.

'I—'

'It's just as well I'm pregnant already,' she continued, her voice growing firmer in the face of his uncertainty.

'And I deserve to be. Wandering round strange men's houses in the middle of the night, wearing nothing but elephant pyjamas.'

He stared down at her, and somehow she managed to get her face in order to smile back at him. Keep it light, her brain was screaming, while all her body wanted to do was rise and…

Nope. Listen to your mind, Dr McKenzie, she ordered herself. It's the only safe course.

She didn't want to be safe. She wanted more! More of Blake Sutherland. More of Blake Sutherland right now!

But he was managing a smile as well, albeit a pretty strained one. His eyes were as wary as hell, and he backed a couple of feet like she wasn't safe.

'I'm sorry.'

'For a kiss?' Her eyes mocked. It wasn't too bad that he was disconcerted, she decided. Normally he was too damned…*concerted* for his own good! 'I refuse to accept your apology. No one apologises for a kiss as good as that one.' She twinkled. 'Together we pack a powerful punch, Dr Sutherland.'

'We do indeed.'

'So you'd best be safely off to bed before we do something we might regret?' She ended on a note of interrogation, and he nodded.

'Yes.'

'Me, too.' She struggled to her feet. He couldn't help himself—his hand came out automatically to help, but after she was steadied he withdrew again. His eyes were like those of a watchful jaguar, a big cat not sure whether what he was watching was hunter or prey.

Nell hesitated. She should bolt for cover, she thought. She should. But…

'You did mean it?' she whispered. 'About caring for the baby if anything happens?'

'I dare say I'd be in a queue. After Emily and Jonas and—'

She didn't let him finish. 'But you did mean it?'

There was a long silence. 'Yes, I did mean it,' Blake said heavily, committed despite himself. 'I did.'

'Thank you,' she whispered, and then, because there was nothing else to say—nothing else to do—she clicked her fingers for Ernest to follow her and she headed for bed.

She stopped at the door and looked back. He looked desperate, she thought. Gorgeous and manly and very, very sexy, but desperate for all that. She so wanted to go to him. To hold him.

But all they had in common was medicine and it was a pretty tenuous link.

'You sleep in tomorrow,' she told him. 'To make up for tonight. I'll do ward rounds and morning surgery.'

'Just morning surgery.'

'Blake…'

'That's all I want,' Blake said heavily. 'Nothing more.' And both of them knew he was talking about something other than medicine.

'Fine.' She was suddenly angry. 'Fine by me, Dr Sutherland.' She clicked her fingers again. Ernest had been dozing underneath the Christmas-tree popcorn, waiting for some to fall on his nose. It was like wishing for the moon, Nell thought bitterly. Or like wanting emotional response from Blake Sutherland. 'Come on, Ernest. We know when we're not wanted.'

Ernest made to follow her, but when he reached her side, he too looked back, as if he would really, really like to stay.

And, amazingly, he was looking at Blake and not at the popcorn. 'Come on, Ernest,' Nell growled again, and cast a last hostile look at the man who was messing with her equanimity. And her dog's equanimity. 'Let's go! We ought to learn when we're not wanted. Heaven knows, we should be good at it by now.'

*　　*　　*

And after that she couldn't get near him. Even with medicine Nell had to fight him every inch of the way, and after a couple of days she was ready to scream.

Blake—graciously—allowed her to conduct morning surgery, which went on for three hours, but that was it. Everything else she tried to do she was politely told to butt out. And sometimes he wasn't even polite. He just ordered.

'Who do you think you are?' she demanded five days before Christmas. They'd just eaten dinner and Blake was about to head out yet again, for the fifth house call for the day. 'I'm being paid as much as you are. What gives you the right to do all the work?'

'You're pregnant.' He was holding himself stiffly away from her, as if she had body odour, and she felt like slapping him. Or throwing the dish she was holding at him. Of all the stupid, pig-headed, obstinate...

'And you're exhausted,' she snapped.

'I'm not exhausted.' He was so matter-of-fact that it was almost impossible to argue with him. 'You're giving me time off.'

'Ha! You do house calls when I'm doing surgery. Time off indeed.'

'It gives me time to run.'

'And that's another thing,' she said darkly. 'You don't need to run for miles every day. It's not normal. It's not even natural.'

'It's healthy.'

'Is it? I believe I was given a certain number of preordained breaths and I'm not going to waste a single one of them jogging.'

'That's the difference between you and me,' he said virtuously, striving for lightness. 'You're indolent.'

'I'm only indolent because you won't let me be anything else.'

'You could spend more time out at your grandparents' house. That way you could move out there earlier.'

'Meaning you could get rid of me earlier?'

'Yes,' he said promptly, and she glowered.

'I can't go out there. They're restumping, and if you think I can live in a house while it's stumpless... Of all the mean things. And it's Christmas, too. Blake Sutherland, you are less than polite.'

'I need to be. It's my only defence.'

'You sound like you're afraid of me.'

'I'm not.'

'And you're looking forward to having Christmas with me?'

'I'm not looking forward to having Christmas with anyone.'

'You, Blake Sutherland, are being too stupid for words.' She rose and slammed her dishes in the sink. One cracked. She stared at it, and then the corners of her mouth creased upward. 'Whoops...'

It was her favourite word, he thought, and why it had the power to twist his thoughts so he hardly knew what he was thinking...

Nell was right. He was being too stupid for words. But something was being threatened here and he didn't know what.

Hell, he was running and he didn't know why.

But Nell suspected. Blake was scared stiff of commitment, she thought. Well, so was she, but it didn't make her mutton-headed.

Blake was a wonderful doctor, she thought time and time again as she watched him at work. Wherever she went there were instances of his skill—and his compassion.

Grace Mayne was a prime example. The old lady came into the surgery the next morning with her hand wrapped in a bloodstained bandage. She'd been filleting fish and had almost filleted herself in the process. The jagged cut needed cleaning and stitching, which took quite a while.

'What on earth are you doing to yourself?' Nell demanded. 'For heaven's sake, after all our trouble with your diabetes... Are you determined to keep us busy?'

'Just stick a stitch in it and don't fuss, girl,' Grace told her. Then she hesitated. 'Actually, I was coming in anyway so Dr Sutherland wouldn't have to come all the way out to my place.'

Nell frowned. 'Why would he come out to your place?' She carefully cleaned the jagged cut, stitched the edges neatly together and tied off her thread. Then, with the task done, she probed some more. 'Your diabetes is stable again, isn't it?'

'Yes, but...' Grace hesitated again and then decided to continue. 'You know my Jack died a couple of months back?'

'Blake told me that.' Her voice gentled. 'I'm sorry.'

'Yeah, well, I didn't take it very well. It seems sometimes that I've lost everyone. Our daughter died of whooping cough when she was just a baby. Mike, our son, was drowned surfing when he was nineteen. And now Jack...' She took a deep breath. 'Anyway, Dr Sutherland comes a couple of times a week—just to make sure I'm OK.'

'And are you OK?' Nell probed gently, and Grace shrugged. Then she smiled. 'Actually, I am,' she said. 'At least, I'm better. The rescue in the boat—it made me feel like I was still useful. And with you in town...' She broke off, as if she feared saying too much, and Nell was left confused. But Grace was moving on.

'It was Dr Sutherland who got me fishing again,' she said, and Nell knew she was changing the subject but didn't know why. 'I've been fishing for garfish for the nursing-home patients—there's a couple of oldies who love them and he knows I'm good at catching them. That's what I was doing when I sliced myself.'

'You were filleting garfish?' Nell was successfully diverted. 'Grace, they're tiny. I've never filleted gars.'

'Yeah, but the old folk don't want bones. I've got time enough to do it and the nurses were good enough to my Jack. It doesn't hurt me to give something in return.' She looked down at the crisp white dressing Nell was placing on her hand and sighed. 'I guess I'll have to wear a glove now.'

'You mean you're going back fishing?'

'It's Christmas in a few days, so fish are in demand, and I might even catch something for myself. It's not worth having turkey on my own. My next-door neighbour goes to his daughter in Sydney and there's no one else.' Her smile slipped, replaced by a pain that was firmly put away. 'Anyway, I reckon I know where I can catch some Moreton Bay bugs. Bugs would be great at Christmas as a meal for one.'

Grace was such a brave old lady, Nell thought. Damn, why was she so alone? She forced herself to smile, following Grace's lead. 'You can really catch Moreton Bay bugs?' She'd had the tiny, lobster-like crustaceans before and they were delicious.

'Cross my heart.'

'You wouldn't like to catch a few for me and Blake?'

'Don't tell me you and Blake are sharing Christmas?'

'Yes. Yes, we are.' At Grace's look of amazement Nell gave her a rueful smile. 'Whether he likes it or not.'

'Then it'd be my pleasure.'

Nell's smile broadened. Grace's pleasure was obvious, but Grace had said she was having Christmas alone. And Nell and Blake...

Nell knew instinctively that Blake would make some excuse to head off for house calls. She'd never see him, and the thought of pulling a solitary Christmas cracker was suddenly less than appealing. 'Grace...'

'Mmm?' Grace was admiring her dressing.

'You wouldn't like to join us for Christmas dinner?'

Her head came up. She was a weathered old fisherwoman, not given to displaying emotion, and she didn't show any now. Instead, her eyes narrowed into a question. 'Why?'

Nell laughed. 'That's a bit rough. It's a very nice invitation.'

'It is, indeed.' She continued to eye Nell and ran a hand through the fading copper of her hair. 'But if you and Blake are having it together…'

'You needn't think you'll be interrupting any tête-à-tête,' Nell said bluntly. 'Blake will find something to keep him busy and I need someone to help me carve the turkey.' She smiled. 'Someone with garfish filleting skills might just know how to do the job.'

Grace gazed down at her hand, and she relaxed. 'You'd let me carve the turkey? That'll keep you busy for the rest of Christmas—bandaging what's left of me.'

'But you'll come?' Nell was pressing, but all of a sudden it seemed important.

'You really are making an effort to be part of this town,' Grace said slowly, and Nell nodded.

'Whether Blake likes it or not. It's home.'

'It never was when you were a child.'

'No, but it should be now. Inviting everyone who needs a Christmas will make me feel more at home.'

'Does Blake know you're doing this?'

'No, but—'

'You don't think you ought to ask him first?'

'No way.' She shook her head. 'He'll find an even bigger reason not to be there. But will you come?'

Grace looked at her for a long, long minute, a strange questioning expression on her face. Finally she nodded, and for some reason it seemed the decision had been momentous. 'Yes, girl, I'll come,' she told her. 'I always was a damned fool for Christmas.'

'Me, too.' Nell fastened the last of the tape and their smiles met. 'Not that I've ever had one.'

'What do you mean?' But then Grace paused, thinking back. 'Your grandparents didn't celebrate Christmas, if I remember.'

'No. And my husband wasn't very much into the Christmas spirit either.'

Grace sighed. 'Oh, girl…' But then she brightened.

'Then it's up to us to make your first proper Christmas great. Who else are you inviting?'

Nell took a deep breath. 'Who do you suggest? Let's make it big. Anyone without someone to share it with them.'

Grace gazed at her, still with that strange half-smile. 'You're giving us a Christmas? After all this town's done to you?'

'What do you mean?'

'I mean you had the pits of a childhood,' Grace said, her voice suddenly harsh. 'No one stood up to your grandparents. Your grandpa was the town doctor. We needed him and you and your mother were treated like dirt. What they did was almost child abuse. We stood by and watched, and now you're organising a Christmas for everyone who needs it.'

'It'll be fun.'

'We don't deserve it.'

'Grace, you've always been kind.'

'No.' She seemed seriously troubled, and Nell laid a hand on her arm.

'Please, Grace. Can we forget my childhood? It's Christmas. I just want to enjoy it. My last Christmas without responsibilities.'

'You're taking on a load of responsibility, even without the baby. You're taking on half of Doc Sutherland's work, and you're taking trouble over us.'

'Grace, please…'

Grace took a deep breath. She met Nell's look head on, and she sighed. 'You really want to do this?'

'I do. It'll be fun.'

'And you don't expect anything in return?'

'What on earth could I want?'

Hmm. Grace was silent for a long time, and then she hauled a blank piece of paper toward her and lifted a pen.

'Christmas,' she said, and her thoughts seemed far away. 'A proper Christmas. How wonderful. Let's make a list.'

But she hadn't answered Nell's question.

CHAPTER NINE

'MRS CONDIE wants to know whether you want Christmas dinner in the hospital.' There were three days to go.

Nell had spent all her spare time organising her Christmas dinner, and now Blake's question caught her unawares. She looked up from wrapping candy canes in red Cellophane, and forced herself to focus.

'You know I've asked a few people. I thought we'd eat here. I'm organising food.'

'Mrs Condie will organise it for you. I don't know how many you have coming but—'

'Grace says maybe twelve.'

'Twelve!'

'There's a lot of lonely people in this town. But I don't want Mrs Condie cooking. The hospital kitchen's cold and sterile and about as unChristmassy as can be. I can do it here. If you help.'

If he helped... He might have known. 'I'm normally busy on Christmas Day.'

She sighed, exasperated. 'Dr Sutherland, that's hogwash, and you know it. In every hospital I've ever been in at Christmas—and, believe me, I've been in a few—there's always a lull at midday. Morning's present-giving and church. Then dinner, which lasts for hours. Then it's time to try out the new skateboard and test the limits of Great-Uncle Donald's peptic ulcer, so our work begins. But that's not until about four. What's your problem?'

His face was shuttered. 'Nell, I didn't ask you to organise this Christmas dinner. It's all very noble of you...'

'Noble. Is that why you think I'm doing it?' She was astounded. 'So I can feel virtuous?'

'I didn't say that.'

'You implied it.' She met his gaze, her green eyes flashing anger. 'You don't think I'll get as much from this as I put in?'

'I don't understand.'

'I mean I want to get involved with this community,' she told him. 'I want people to like me and I want to like them. In short, I want emotional attachment—something you're running scared of.'

'I'm not.'

'Don't kid yourself. You are. And for heaven's sake, what harm can it do? There's twelve of the town's old folk coming to Christmas dinner. They want a good time and so do you. And it could happen. If you let it.'

But his face was closed. As far as Blake was concerned, the conversation was ended. 'I'll eat with you if I can.'

'Gee, thanks.'

'I'm sorry.' And suddenly he was. He looked at her face and thought he'd hurt her. She was trying to hide it, but there it was. Hell, he'd hurt her and she'd had enough kicks already. But she wanted something he wasn't able to give.

She wanted commitment—not just to the town's elderly, but to her.

And he couldn't give it.

'I'll try and share my meal with you,' he said gently, and her eyes flew to his, her temper flaring.

'There's no need to patronise me.'

'I didn't mean—'

'Mean it or not, it reeked of patronising. Blake Sutherland, we're stuck together for Christmas so you may as well be civil about it.'

We're stuck together... He stared at her for a long moment, and then he spun on his heel and stalked away— because he didn't have the faintest clue how to deal with what was happening. Because he didn't even know what was happening! And he didn't want to know.

*   *   *

For how long were they stuck together? he wondered desperately as he tried to sleep that night. It was getting harder and harder to sleep. Nell was just through the wall, and the memories of that kiss were enough to keep him staring at the ceiling for so long he thought he'd go nuts.

She could well be here for the whole month. Over two more weeks and maybe longer. He'd driven past her house a few days back and seen it in its unstumped glory. It had broken windows, there were boards missing from the verandah and the whole house was layered with dust. In this town things moved slowly. She'd be lucky if it was finished by the time her baby was born!

How would he cope with that?

He wouldn't have to, he told himself hastily. She'd go to Blairglen for her baby's birth. She needed to go there at least two weeks before the baby was due, so that gave him an end point of five weeks at the latest. In five weeks he could be rid of her.

But how would he cope for that long?

'Please, let it be shorter,' he pleaded to the silence as he waited for elusive sleep. He didn't want her near. He didn't want her in this house—he didn't want her dog, her furniture, her silly damned Christmas tree. He wanted to be alone!

He slept at last, but if he could have known it his prayers were being answered right now. Because out on the bluff, the town was very much still awake.

The population of Sandy Ridge was working on making Dr Sutherland alone again.

'Dr Sutherland...'

It was late afternoon on Christmas Eve and they were nearing the end of Theatre. Scott Henderson had presented that morning complaining of abdominal tenderness. He'd seen Nell, Nell had admitted him and they'd watched for a couple of hours, hoping it might settle. Then suddenly there'd been rebound. A grumbling appendix had burst and a procedure they'd hoped he could have been spared until after Christmas was suddenly urgent.

At least such an operation was possible now in Sandy Ridge. With Nell there, they'd been able to operate fast and effectively. The appendix had been removed, the peritoneal cavity had been cleaned, a heavy dosage of antibiotics was already being fed in through the intravenous drip and Scott had every chance of being able to eat a Christmas dinner. He'd be stiff and sore, but he should be fine.

Now there was only the wound to finish suturing. Blake was concentrating totally—that way he didn't have to chat. If he chatted with anyone it had to be with Nell, and that seemed impossible. So Nell chatted with the theatre staff as she started to reverse the anaesthetic, and Blake was left to indulge in what was starting to seem like sullen silence.

For heaven's sake, he was behaving like a spoiled schoolkid, he thought as he sutured. He was being unreasonable. Stupid. And why?

He didn't know why. He only knew that to hold himself apart was the only way he knew of protecting himself—so when Marion put her head around the door to call him, he was almost relieved to be called. If he was needed, then Nell could take over and he could get out of there.

'Yes?'

'There's been an accident,' Marion told him. 'One of the builders. Out at Nell's place.'

'What sort of accident?'

'Collapse of a part of a wall. There's a couple of men trapped.'

Hell!

Nell was staring. 'How can a wall have collapsed?' she asked, puzzled. 'They weren't doing any major structural work.'

'They're reblocking.'

'That shouldn't make a wall collapse.'

'You don't know the tradesmen in this town,' Blake said grimly. He tied off the last stitch and motioned to Donald to apply the dressing. 'These guys have been inbreeding for generations and sometimes I think if they had one neuron collectively it'd be lonely.' He motioned toward Scott, and he was already stripping off his theatre gown. 'Can you take over here?'

'Of course.' But Nell bit her lip. 'Blake, it's my house. I'm coming, too.'

'I need to go straight away.' It was as if he was desperate to get away from her, Nell thought grimly, but he was right. He had to leave and she couldn't go yet.

'I'll follow. As soon as I've reversed the anaesthetic and Scott's stable…'

'I'll contact you if I need you.' Blake let his eyes rest on the bump of her pregnancy. 'You've had a big day, and it'll be dirty and dangerous out there.'

'It's my house,' she said belligerently, and his eyes softened.

'Yeah, I know, but you're tired. I'll let you know the damage as soon as I can.'

'I'm coming. As soon as Scott—'

'OK.' He held up his hands in surrender. There wasn't time for arguing. 'I'll see you soon.'

She *was* tired. Half an hour later Nell was in her little car, travelling out toward her house and hoping desperately that there was nothing major wrong, but overriding her problem was the wave of fatigue that was threatening to overwhelm her.

The last few days had been busier than she'd ever expected them to be, she thought as she drove. There'd been all the organisation for Christmas, and, as well as that, she seemed to have been needed medically.

She grimaced as she rounded the headland and steered the car up the long driveway to the house. Blake had insisted that she still only do morning surgery, so she should have had heaps of time. She should have been out at her house every day, seeing what the builders were doing.

But it seemed like every time she went toward her car there'd been someone hurrying toward her, or the phone would ring and it would be…something. Marg Connors wanting a woman-to-woman chat about how to tell the facts of life to her daughter. Grace wanting to talk about the merits of installing a security system so if she fell at night she could get help. Bob wanting to know whether his mother should move into a nursing home. It was always things that might normally merit a trip to the doctor, if the doctor had been less pressed than Blake.

The town had elected her their alternative doctor, Nell thought as she drove, and she should be grateful. She was sparing Blake work. But now she didn't have a clue what was happening to her house and her back ached with a dull, sickening throb.

She'd been standing too long over surgery, she thought. She should have sat to give the anaesthetic, and now she had to cope with a collapsed house and injured men—and a turkey that needed stuffing before she went to bed that night!

'Merry Christmas, Dr McKenzie,' she told herself wryly as she drew to a halt. 'After all, you asked for this…' And then she stopped, and stared up at the house.

It wasn't the same house.

She must be dreaming. But she wasn't. The house was standing where it had stood for a hundred years—her grandparents' house—but what a difference!

Gone were the broken windows, the peeling paintwork, the tilting verandah. This was a house that hadn't been seen for years—in fact, Nell didn't remember her house ever looking like this.

From her grandparents' time the house had been painted a dull mission brown. Now the house was the palest of soft yellows, almost cream but not quite, and it was trimmed with a grey-blue that took its inspiration from the sea. The windows were spotlessly clean and there wasn't a broken pane. They swung wide to the sea and they were laced with

curtains that Nell had never seen, each of the same blue
with the softest cream on their inmost border.

What else? The wide verandah had a new railing. The
floorboards were polished redwood, smooth and gorgeous.
Nell climbed out of the car and crossed the verandah, still
feeling as if she were dreaming.

She hadn't been near the place for a week, she thought
dazedly. When she'd rung the builder she'd been told he
was struggling to get things done. He'd sounded totally
unorganised and Nell had despaired of moving out of
Blake's before the baby was born.

And now she could.

But…the wall? The collapsed wall? Where on earth…?

It didn't exist. Of course it didn't exist. It had simply
been a ruse to get both doctors here. Instead of casualties,
as Nell opened the wide front door there were a hundred
people—maybe more. Balloons. Banners. Huge signs.
'Welcome home, Nell. Welcome home!'

She couldn't believe it—but they were all watching her,
waiting for her reaction. Blake was there, too, with a very
strange expression on his face. He must have been surprised
as well, she thought. They'd kept this a secret from both
of them. People were smiling at her. Laughing.

Blake wasn't smiling.

He should be. This meant she could get out of his life
earlier than either had dreamed possible.

She could go now.

'What do you think?' It was Grace, the lovely wrinkled
old fisherwoman, still in paint-spattered overalls as if she'd
just this minute put the finishing touches to the walls.
Which indeed she had.

Nell turned to her, and hugged her hard. There were tears
glistening in the old lady's eyes, and they were mirrored in
Nell's.

'Was this your idea?'

'It might have been,' Grace said noncommittally, and
Nell knew it had.

'It's beautiful.'

It was all beautiful. The inside had been worked on as well as the outside. From the doors leading from the sitting room, Nell could see that every room had been painted and the floors and furniture washed and polished till they shone. All her grandparents' furniture looked wonderful...

Including...

'You've brought back the stuff I took to Blake's.'

'It's yours.' The ambulancemen were there, too. Bob and Henry were laughing at her shock and enjoying themselves hugely. 'You can't believe the trouble the townsfolk have had keeping you away from this place for the past few days—the complaints they've had to make up to distract you. We've worked in shifts to keep you away from here. Scott's appendix was a blessing. And we thought Blake'd hardly mind if we shifted your furniture back home. After all, he's got his house to himself again. Losing the odd sofa'd hardly matter.'

'You left him the tree?' Suddenly it seemed absurdly important that they had. He had to have something. He needed his Christmas angels!

But they had left them so she could stop worrying. 'We made you your own,' Grace told her, motioning to the corner where Christmas lights twinkled. Her arm was still around Nell's in an out-of-character display of affection. 'The town thought...well, you've been home for less than two weeks and already you've risked your skin saving one of us, and now you're putting on a fantastic Christmas for us oldies. Nell, we never stood up for you against your grandparents. We figured the least we could do was to see you had Christmas in your own home.'

'Oh, Grace...' She gazed around at them. At her people. *Her* people. And they beamed back, hugely satisfied with her pleasure.

Except Blake. He was standing on the sidelines, watching but not saying a word. Her gaze swung to his face and found his eyes creased, as if they were puzzled.

He was puzzled. Not pleased. Not displeased. Just... puzzled. Why?

He'd have his home to himself for Christmas, she thought. That should please him.

'I'm sorry about your furniture,' she said softly, and he managed a smile. His gaze moved from Nell's face to Grace's, and then back again, and the trace of puzzlement remained. She didn't understand it, but finally he dragged himself back to what she'd said. The furniture. Right.

'I can live without your furniture,' he told her. 'I have for the past two years.'

There was a pause—a moment when silence fell over the whole room. It was as if the room were witnessing a declaration.

He could live without her furniture. He could live without her. Of course he could. Why had she ever imagined differently?

After all, she was plain Nell McKenzie, a woman who was pregnant with another man's baby, a woman who was so different from his beautiful Sylvia that...

She blinked. What was she thinking of? The town's people had just given her this house and here she was fantasising about things that were totally ridiculous. Like a relationship with Blake.

He didn't need her, she told herself. He didn't want her, and if she gave any hint to the contrary then she'd make their working relationship untenable. When her baby was born she wanted part-time work here. She wanted to be his part-time partner.

Not his full-time love.

Or rather she did want that—very, very much—but she knew very well that trying for the second would destroy completely her chances of the first. So she just had to get on with it. With a wrench she forced her gaze away from Blake, back to the townspeople surrounding her.

'I suppose you haven't all gathered here to haul some injured builder from under a collapsed wall?'

There was general laughter and then someone handed her a glass of champagne, someone else started to play on her grandmother's piano, a fiddler tuned his instrument to the piano—and the party to end all parties began. A party to welcome Dr Nell McKenzie back amongst her own.

Blake left. Pleading the excuse that he needed to check Scott, he gave it an hour and then headed back to town. He did it via a detour. The beach was calling. The sea...

He desperately wanted to run. Desperately! He parked on the headland and stared down at the moonlit ribbon of sand stretching away to the horizon. He wanted to run and run, and never stop running. Away from here. He wanted to leave! He didn't want Nell staying in this town, disturbing his precious solitude.

She wouldn't be disturbing it now, he told himself. She'd no longer be sleeping just through the wall from him. She'd be in *her* house. He wouldn't have to see her. She'd be gone.

But she'd still be...there.

Damn. Damn, damn and damn. His hand thumped down onto the steering-wheel and he hit the hooter without meaning to. A bunch of dopey seagulls squawked their indignation at being rudely wakened and then settled again to their nightly roost.

He should go. Scott was waiting.

The beeper was on his belt. The nurses would beep him if he was needed.

Hell, why didn't they beep him? He was going nuts.

Finally he turned on the engine and forced himself to steer homewards. Ernest would still be at the apartment, he thought suddenly. Everything else of Nell's had been moved. He'd seen that she had it all—the energetic towns-folk had shifted everything, even the food for tomorrow's Christmas dinner. But her dog hadn't been at the party. They must have thought so many people in a strange place night upset him so they'd leave Ernest for Nell to collect later.

The thought was good. Ernest would still be still there, so she'd have to come to…

'Oh, for heaven's sake, Sutherland!' He didn't want Nell to come. He didn't want anyone! He was sure of it. But it was with a heavy heart that he headed back toward the town.

Toward the flat. Toward Ernest. Toward all that was left of Nell McKenzie.

When Blake woke it was Christmas, and Nell wasn't there. He lay and stared at the ceiling for a long time and tried not to think just how 'not there' it felt. Which was pretty much overwhelming.

Six a.m. There was plenty of time before he had to get up. He'd scheduled surgery from ten to eleven for urgent cases—the earaches and fevers that couldn't wait. He needed to do a ward round before then, but they'd look askance if he came in now, so the next couple of hours were his to do with as he wished. But he didn't wish to do anything.

He'd run, he thought. That'd be a good start to the day. Having made his decision, he threw off the bedcovers and headed for the living room, to discover Ernest fast asleep under the Christmas tree.

'What on earth are you doing?' he demanded. The dog was lying on his back, staring up at the tree like it personally had robbed him. 'You weren't hoping Father Christmas would drop in, were you?'

Maybe the dog had been hoping just that. The gaze that Ernest turned on him—reproachfulness personified—said he certainly wasn't happy. Blake sighed and crossed to the fridge.

'OK, I don't see why Santa should desert both of us.' There was a portion of leg ham in the fridge—small enough for one person to demolish over Christmas. All the won-

derful food that had been there the day before had been
taken out to Nell's but they'd left him enough to get by.
Just.

'You'll be eating your main meal with us so there's no
need to leave you all the trimmings,' he'd been told by
Grace, and he could only agree, even if he didn't intend to
eat anywhere near Nell.

So there was ham, eggs, a bowl of strawberries and not
a lot else. Blake sliced the ham from the bone, ate a slice
himself—well, he should do something to celebrate
Christmas—and then he offered the bone to Ernest. 'Merry
Christmas,' he told him.

But Ernest wasn't in a Christmas mood. He sniffed the
bone and sighed heavily. Slowly, deliberately, he carried it
to where the plain rug had replaced Nell's Turkish ones on
the living-room floor. Without looking at Blake again, the
dog scraped the rug back, deposited the bone underneath
and proceeded to lie on top of it.

His body language was unmistakable. I'm miserable
now. I appreciate the gesture and maybe I'll eat it later, but
I'm too sad to eat just yet.

'You're supposed to eat it now,' Blake told him, lifting
a piece of ham and biting. 'Like this. It's Christmas now.'

But Ernest wasn't happy and Blake knew exactly how
he felt.

'You're missing Nell?' Blake stooped to pat the velvety
head. 'I thought she'd come and get you.' He had, too.
Blake had lain awake until the small hours, thinking that
Nell might sleep here. Her bed was still made up and her
dog was here and… And he was here!

Damn, that'd make no difference at all. He was being
ridiculous.

'How about you come down to the beach and run with
me?' Blake enquired, and Ernest looked so unenthusiastic
that he almost laughed. Almost.

'OK.' Blake knew when he was beaten. 'Give me five
minutes and we'll take your damned bone and we'll give

the pair of you back to your mistress.' And then he'd really be alone for Christmas—which was the way he wanted it. Wasn't it?

Maybe.

In the end it was eight before he reached Nell's, which was maybe just as well as Nell would hardly have appreciated a six a.m. wake-up call. But he'd been delayed. Jodie Farmer had sat all night in a steam tent with her croupy baby and had waited until dawn to bring her baby in.

'Because I know last night was a big night and I didn't want to bother you. Did you enjoy the party?'

'Very much, thank you.'

Jodie had surveyed him with care. She was almost as wide as she was high, big-hearted with it and as sharp as a tack. 'You and Doc McKenzie had a fight, then?'

'No. Why would we fight?'

'You didn't stay out there?'

'Of course I didn't. It's Nell's house, not mine.'

She wasn't satisfied. 'But you still fancy her?'

'Of course I don't.'

'No "of course" about it,' she said bluntly. 'My old man put ten quid on the pair of you being married by the time her baby's born.' She grinned. 'Got long odds, too, so we'd appreciate it if you'd oblige.'

'Not even for you, Jodie,' he said, goaded. Good grief!

'So what's wrong with being married?' Jodie looked down at the baby in her arms and she grinned. 'Last night was the pits but we wouldn't give her back, and me and Daryl think marriage is great! And now you'll even stick Lily in hospital so we can have Christmas dinner in peace. Bliss.'

'You'd be well served if I didn't admit her.'

'Then I'd fall asleep on top of her and you know it. Daryl was out all night, fishing, so he's no help. I'll see her settled, crawl into bed with my hubby and wake in time to have Christmas dinner with my in-laws. Marriage is great, Doc Sutherland. You ought to try it.'

'No, thanks.'

'You couldn't be talked into it?'

The woman was impossible. 'I've been married already,' he said curtly, but even that wasn't enough to shut her up.

'Doc McKenzie's different,' she told him, refusing to be silent. 'She's special.'

'So was my wife.'

'Yeah, well.' She shrugged, but she still grinned. 'Not from what I've heard, but have it your own way. I'm still backing Daryl's bet. I might even have a flutter myself.'

'You'll lose your money,' Blake told her, striving desperately to bring this crazy conversation to an end. It was at times like this that he wanted to be something other than a doctor. Like a hermit! But he lifted Jodie's baby into his arms and felt a jabbing ache of uncertainty. Lily's tiny face was so innocent. So trusting.

'Hey, you're ripe for marriage,' Jodie said, watching him and smiling.

'I've got all I can cope with, looking after everyone else's kids,' he retorted. He forced himself back to the business at hand. 'Her breathing's still a bit blocked, Jodie, so we will admit her.'

'I knew you would.' Then, before he knew what she intended, she grabbed him—and her baby—in an all-enveloping hug. 'I think you're the greatest,' she told him. 'And so's Dr McKenzie. So off you go and win Daryl's bet for me. Right now.'

CHAPTER TEN

THOROUGHLY disgruntled, Blake walked up the front steps of Nell's house and hoped she was awake. He'd offload the dog and be out of here, he told himself. Fast.

He knocked on the back screen, Ernest by his side, but they were met by silence. He knocked again and the door swung inwards. Instead of Nell, though, he was confronted with Wendy Gunner.

Wendy was Aaron's wife. He'd seen her the day before at her husband's hospital bedside, with her three children in tow. Things had been looking good for her—her husband was recovering fast—and she'd been bright, cheerful and bubbly.

She was none of that now. She looked pale and drawn. She was still dressed in her nightwear and her two littlest children were clinging to her side.

'Wendy!'

'Dr Sutherland!'

His stomach lurched somewhere toward his feet as he heard her fear. His hands came out and gripped hers, holding hard. 'Wendy, what's wrong? Where's Nell?'

'She's…she's in the bathroom.'

'The baby…' Hell, the baby!

But it wasn't the baby. Wendy gave a choking sob and shook her head. 'No. It's not the baby. It's Jason.'

'Your Jason?' He didn't understand. Jason was her eight-year-old. 'What's going on?'

'He got a bike for Christmas.' Another sob. 'The kids have been up for hours. Jason took the bike straight out onto the gravel drive and while I wasn't looking he stuck a plank on some bricks to make a jump. Of all the stupid things…

And now his leg… You should see it. There's blood and gravel and he's ripped his pyjamas and I know I should be in there helping, but all of a sudden I felt sick and I couldn't…' She buried her face in her hands.

'Hey, Wendy.' Blake's arms came around and held her. He could guess what was happening. While her husband's life had been in danger and afterwards, Wendy had been fantastic. She'd held herself composed and cheerful and optimistic throughout.

But now the accumulated strain of keeping cheerful for Aaron's sake and the after-effects of the terror had proved too much. One damaged knee was all it had taken to push her over the edge.

Blake needed to find out how badly the child was hurt. There were murmurs coming from the bathroom, but Wendy needed help first.

'Kyle.' Blake looked down at the second of the children. Kyle was six years old and was lost in the face of his mother's distress. Blake knelt and met him at eye level. 'Kyle, your mother's upset. Jason's sore knee has made her sad. But there's nothing to worry about. I bet Dr McKenzie is bandaging it really well, and I want to help her, so do you think that if your mum sits on the sofa right here, you and Christy could give her a cuddle?'

Kyle considered the matter gravely. His thumb was permanently stuck in his mouth and his eyes were huge. He stared up at his mother in bewilderment.

'Mummy's crying.'

'That's why she needs a cuddle.' Blake turned to the four-year-old. 'Christy, can you help?'

Wendy's daughter was made of sterner stuff than her brother. She nodded at once.

'Sit down, Mummy,' she ordered, and Blake grinned and put his hands on Wendy's shoulders and propelled her to sit.

'Now cuddle,' he ordered, and Christy did just that. After a moment's doubt, Kyle followed.

'Don't you let your mother up,' Blake ordered as Wendy's

arms came out in an instinctive reaction to hold them both close. 'She's not to move.' He motioned to the dog who'd followed him hopefully into the house. There were good smells coming from here. Christmas smells. Food smells. It was enough to make a dog really optimistic. 'If she stands up, you tell Ernest to lick her,' Blake told the children. 'That'll fix her.'

'Does he bite?' Kyle asked, diverted from his mother for a moment.

'No. His specialty is licking. Very, very wetly.'

'He'll lick our mummy?'

'Only if you let her up.'

It appealed enormously to the two children. They stared at Ernest for a long moment, Ernest stared back, and they got the message. They got on with the important task of mother-cuddling.

Blake found Nell, with the little boy sitting on towels on the bathroom floor. She'd ripped the pyjama leg aside to reveal a nasty gravel rash. By the look of Jason's face— stoic rather than in pain—she must have given him a local anaesthetic, but it was a big job. He'd scraped not only his knee but his leg almost down to his ankle.

'Well, Jason Gunner. You've made a right proper mess,' Blake growled as he entered the room, and Nell looked up with relief. She'd been kneeling on the floor as she worked, and by the look of it, the floor wasn't at all comfortable.

'Blake...' There was no hiding her relief, and Blake felt a small surge of satisfaction. Actually, quite a large surge.

'Can I help?'

'If you would.' She winced, grabbed the towel rail and hauled herself to her feet before he could help. Her hand moved to the small of her back and she grimaced again. 'Operating on the floor when you're this far pregnant is hardly fun. I should have used the kitchen table—except that the turkey's using it.' She managed a smile, but it was a wan one. 'I've given Jason a local anaesthetic so we can get all the gravel out without hurting him, but I'd be very grateful if you could take over.'

Blake didn't hesitate. He crossed to the basin and started washing. 'Of course. What on earth was Wendy thinking of, coming to you?'

'It's Christmas,' Nell said simply. 'They're my next-door neighbours and they didn't want to disturb you.'

Right. It was a major hazard of being a country GP. Patients thought it was somehow easier for all concerned to land on the doctor's front doorstep rather than come to the surgery. It wasn't and, by the look of Nell's face, she'd been feeling the strain.

'Not up to taking on my full workload?' he asked, and she flushed. Damn. Why had he said that? She was distressed, he thought, and it was he who'd distressed her.

'I'm sorry. That was uncalled for.'

'It's true. I'm useless. I'm not usually—'

'Usually you're a really fine doctor,' he told her, meeting her eyes and smiling—trying to make her smile back. 'But kneeling on the floor when you have ten-ton Tess aboard is hardly sensible.'

That made her indignant—which was just the reaction he'd been angling for. 'Hey, my baby's hardly ten-ton Tess.'

'He looks like it—doesn't he, Jason?' Blake had swiftly washed his hands and was already stooping over the injured knee. 'Holy cow, how much gravel did you get in here, Jason Gunner? You must have been travelling at a hundred miles an hour. It must be some bike that Santa left.'

'It's red,' Jason told him proudly. 'And it's got little wheels so I can do heaps of tricks.'

'Well, you write a letter to Santa and tell him he forgot knee and elbow pads,' Blake said sternly. 'What was Santa thinking of?' Then he relented. 'You didn't hurt your bike?'

'No.' Jason managed a gap-toothed grin. 'I checked it before I had a look at my knee.'

'You're born to be a Formula One driver.' Then Blake glanced up at Nell and his smile faded. She was almost as white-faced as Jason. 'Go and make yourself a cup of tea, Dr McKenzie,' he suggested. 'I can finish here.'

'I don't need a cup of tea.'

'Well, ten-ton Tess might.'

'Is your baby really ten tons?' Jason asked, interested, and Nell managed a smile.

'I hope not, but he sure feels that way at the moment.'

'When exactly is your due date?' Blake asked, focussing in sudden concern. The baby had dropped, he thought. Nell looked different. The baby was no longer a neat bundle around her midriff. Had it dropped in preparation for delivery? Surely not.

'February eight. There's a good six weeks to go.'

'You're sure of your dates?'

'Of course I'm sure. I'm a doctor, aren't I?'

'You've had an ultrasound?'

'No, but—'

'But nothing. Hell, Nell...'

'Do you mind?' she snapped, motioning to the boy. 'Concentrate on Jason.'

'Sorry, Jase.' Blake turned back to what he was doing. 'You didn't hear what I just said.'

'Hell?' Jason enquired, and Blake smiled.

'It's not a word to say in front of ladies. I only said it because I was provoked.'

'What's provoked?'

'Something Dr McKenzie is very good at. She's a very provoking lady.'

Jason thought that through. 'Does provoking mean pretty?'

'That's part of it.' He'd determined to keep his mind on the job. There was only a tiny area of the wound left uncleaned. He scrubbed the top layer, scrubbed harder and then used tweezers to remove the last of it. Finally he looked around to find a dressing and Nell placed it into his hand, unasked.

Her presence was strangely disconcerting. 'I thought I told you to go and have a cup of tea,' he growled.

'I told you I didn't want one.'

'See?' Blake demanded of his patient. 'Provoking. Provoking, provoking and even more provoking.'

'She is pretty,' Jason agreed, and Blake grinned.

'She's pretty fat.' Ignoring Nell's indignant gasp, he came to the point he needed to focus on next. 'You saw Emily last week?' he demanded of Nell.

'Yes. Why do you ask? You know I drove across to visit her.'

'And she examined you?'

'She says everything's fine.'

'But she examined you?'

'Yes!'

'And she agrees with your dates?'

'Why wouldn't she? I know I'm right.'

'Have you got a bassinet yet?' Jason asked, interested. 'Cos there's one at my place.'

'I won't need a bassinet for ages,' Nell said, a trace of desperation in her tone. 'I'll worry about that when I stop working—in two weeks!'

'You're exhausted now,' Blake told her.

'No. Yes! Maybe I am, but only because I danced until the small hours last night, and then I had to stuff the turkey and lay the table.'

And Jason was on her doorstep to stop her sleeping in, Blake thought—but she must already have been up and dressed. She was looking great, in a gorgeous crimson maternity dress. It was a simple sundress with shoestring shoulder straps, cut low across her breast and then flaring in soft folds to mid-calf.

She was pretty, Jason had decreed, and Blake agreed entirely.

'What else have you got left to do?' he asked, fitting white gauze across Jason's knee and lower leg.

'Not much.'

'You have a dozen people coming for Christmas dinner. That's hardly not much.'

'They're all bringing something. My job's the turkey and the roast potatoes. Everything else is done—oh, except the brandy sauce.'

'So after the brandy sauce you can have a rest before everyone gets here.'

'I guess.' She sounded doubtful as she glanced at her watch.

'Right.' Blake lifted Jason and set him on his feet. 'That's you fixed—which gives me time to help Dr McKenzie with the brandy sauce before morning surgery.'

'Are you having Christmas dinner with Dr McKenzie?' Jason asked, and Nell butted in before he could answer.

'Of course he is.'

'Maybe…'

'We're having Christmas dinner in Dad's room at the hospital,' Jason said proudly, oblivious to the tension that was suddenly filling the bathroom. 'But afterwards… If I promise not to fall off, can I ride my bike over to show it to you?'

'We'd love to see it.' Nell smiled at Blake. 'Wouldn't we?'

Blake glowered. 'I don't know whether I'll be here. I don't know how busy I'll be.'

'You can't be too busy for Christmas dinner,' Jason said, shocked.

'We'll see.'

They took Jason out to the hall to discover Wendy had pulled herself together and was in control again. Just. 'I'm really grateful,' she told them. 'And, Nell, I'm so sorry for disturbing you on Christmas morning.'

'Think nothing of it.' Nell was watching Wendy's face, taking in the strain around her eyes. 'It's been a crazy Christmas for you.'

'Yes.' Wendy faltered, but tried to keep her voice bright. 'It's an odd one. Just me and the kids. We were supposed to go to my sister's in Blairglen. All the family are going.'

'Instead of which, you're pandering to the invalid.'

'It feels funny.' Wendy blinked, determined to hold back the tears which were just behind her eyes. 'When Aaron was hurt, the family offered to come here, but my sister's eight months pregnant and I thought it wasn't fair. I mean…' Her eyes flew to Nell's tummy. 'Well, eight months or not, she could have it any minute.'

'Hey, I'm not due for six weeks,' Nell said decisively. 'And first babies are always late.'

'Yeah.' But both Blake and Wendy were looking at Nell's tummy like a coiled snake.

'Oh, cut it out, the pair of you.' Nell managed a laugh. 'Wendy, are you saying that after you leave hospital you're going home alone?'

'With the kids. Yes.'

'You'd better come here, then,' Nell told her. 'It's open house for anyone who can sing Christmas carols. We don't mind if you come late and have eaten heaps already. You can help finish the brandy sauce.'

'I couldn't.' But it was obviously enticing. 'Oh, Nell…'

'I'd love you to. We both would. Wouldn't we, Blake?' Nell grinned and tucked her arm into Blake's, whether he liked it or not, making them an instant couple. 'The average age of my guests is about a hundred and six. I suspect one tablespoon of my brandy sauce and they'll be out for the count, so I depend on you and Blake to keep me company.' She twinkled at Wendy and then she turned her smile on Blake. 'And to help me wash up.'

Wendy smiled back. 'If you put it like that.' She looked a question at Blake. 'And if you're coming, too…'

He was stuck. They were all watching him, two women and three children, their faces bright with expectation. And Nell was by his side, holding his arm in hers and smiling up at him. Her body was warm and close and… And it was suddenly all too much.

'I'll come if I can,' he said, goaded, and Nell grinned.

'What a very polite way of accepting.'

'It's the best I can do.'

It was only a meal, for heaven's sake. Why did it feel like he was signing his life away? *I'll come if I can...* Heaven knew that he couldn't.

Wendy took her children home, the four of them skipping down the track with Jason barely limping.

'Kids are amazing,' Blake said, watching them go. 'You and me'd be in bed after falling like that.'

'You think Jason would go to bed when there's a new bike to be ridden?' Nell laughed. 'I wouldn't be surprised if he's back, having the other knee bandaged, before nightfall.'

'He'll be back anyway—for your party.'

'He will, too.'

'It's too much for you,' Blake said savagely, watching her face. Despite the gorgeousness of her crimson dress, she still looked pale. 'Hell, Nell, why do you—?'

'Do you mind not swearing at Christmas?'

'I'll swear if I want to.'

'Ernest is shocked.'

'Ernest is concentrating entirely on turkey, and stop changing the subject. Nell...'

'Are you going to help me with the brandy sauce?' she demanded. 'Or are you just planning to stand around, getting in the way? Because if you are, I promise I'll hang mistletoe on your nose. And there's six widows coming to my dinner, and they all know what mistletoe's for.'

Blake smiled but he was still worried. 'Nell...'

'Just shut up and work,' she told him, pushing him into the kitchen. 'Do you know how to separate eggs?'

'Separate eggs. You mean one from the other?'

'And you a surgeon,' she told him, exasperated. She plonked a carton of eggs in front of him. 'I'll show you one, and you do the other eleven.'

'A full dozen! How much brandy sauce do we need?' he demanded, startled, and she chuckled.

'How long's a piece of string? Goodness knows.'

'So what's it got in it?' He picked up the recipe book,

and saw it written in a child's handwriting. 'Where did you get this?'

And for a moment she hesitated. 'Um…'

His attention was caught. 'Don't tell me it's a secret.'

'No.'

'Then what?'

'It was written on a slip of paper tucked into one of my mother's books. I found it stowed in the garage with everything else of my mother's. Heaven knows where she got it, because my grandmother certainly never made it, but now it's one of the few things left to me.' She put a cream container on the table and reached for an apron. 'So I guess you could say it's a family recipe. *My* family.'

Blake felt his gut wrench at that, a feeling he was starting to recognise. She'd had so little, and she could have so much more—but, then, for Nell to have more, he'd have to give. So what was he thinking of?

He knew what he was thinking of. He knew what he wanted. He wanted Nell to have a family, and he wanted that family to be him! But for him to be Nell's family he'd have to break down barriers that had taken him years to build, and he didn't want that. Did he?

No. No and no and no. Definitely not.

'If you don't hurry and break those eggs, you'll miss morning surgery,' she was saying. 'Mind, I've done half your work for you.'

With a start he jerked himself back to the job at hand. Brandy sauce. The important things in life. Right.

She was supposed to be sleeping. After Blake left, Nell tried to settle. Instead, she wandered around the house like someone lost, Ernest trailing behind her. Her back still ached, she was weary and she was downright miserable.

Would he come back? Even though he'd promised, she didn't think so. He'd find some urgent medical need and he'd phone with an excuse that she couldn't fault.

'You're a fool, Nell McKenzie,' she told herself for the

fortieth time. 'You have a house. A dog. Friends. People coming to Christmas dinner who you care about. What else do you want?'

Blake.

The answer was written across her heart as if it had been branded by fire. She wanted him so much, and she was stupid, stupid, stupid. Because Blake didn't want her. He didn't want anyone, and she simply had to accept that and get on with her life—as best she could.

But she certainly couldn't sleep.

'Merry Christmas!'

Ethel Norris was the first to arrive, carrying a boiler almost wider than she was. The pudding lay on the back seat of her car as Nell came out to greet her, and it was bigger than a basketball. 'I know I'm early but if the pudding doesn't go on soon it won't be ready.'

'What a pudding!' Nell lifted it and groaned with the weight. Her back stabbed again with the pain she was starting to expect. She hid her grimace as best she could. 'Heck, Ethel, what did you put in this?' Drat, what was wrong with her? Her legs felt like jelly.

But Ethel was too busy to notice. 'Everything but the kitchen sink.' The big woman beamed. 'I've never made such a pudding. It should have been made a couple of months ago, but with this party planned just this week I had to put more brandy in to compensate.' Her beam widened, and Nell thought back to the miserable Ethel she'd met when she'd first come back to town, and she could only wonder.

'Hey, and I've lost two more pounds,' Ethel told her, guessing where Nell's thoughts were headed. 'How good's that?'

'You're not dieting today!'

'No fear. No, Dr McKenzie, I'm following your advice and very good advice it is, too. Now, let's get this pudding on the stove and see what else needs to be done.'

Soon after Ethel came Grace, bearing trays of Moreton

Bay bugs, gleaming in their crimson glory, with bowls of home-made tartare sauce and slices of fresh lime.

Then old Norman Harper arrived with oysters, Harriet Walsingham with salads made from her own garden—a Harriet complete with pacemaker on board and details of her Very Interesting Heart Surgery—Bert with baby potatoes dug that morning, Marg with fresh peas, the ancient Toby with a whole bucket of fresh cream he'd scooped off his magnificent Jerseys' milk, Elsie with strawberries, Clare with home-made chocolates…

By the time they sat down to dinner the table was groaning, and Nell looked around at the sea of smiling faces and thought, Why wouldn't you do something like this? If not for this, all these people would have sat down to Christmas dinner alone, and they'd have been collectively miserable.

The only dampener to her spirits was that Blake still wasn't here, and she couldn't stop thinking of him. Drat the man. He hadn't even phoned. Somewhere he was eating his Christmas dinner alone. He'd be in the hospital kitchen, she thought, or in his apartment with his boneless ham and his one punnet of strawberries. She wished suddenly that she'd sent some of this food over to him. She couldn't bear that here there was so much and he had so little.

But he had to make the first move himself, she told herself fiercely, and he wouldn't. He wanted to be solitary!

'Pull my cracker,' Tom told her, and then Grace and Ethel carried in the turkey between them. The bird was golden brown and so succulent Nell could almost taste it before she raised it to her mouth.

'Happy Christmas,' Grace said, and raised her champagne flute across the table to Nell. 'Welcome home, Dr McKenzie. Welcome to your first proper Christmas at Sandy Ridge, and may there be many more.'

There were cheers all around, and Grace was watching her with a look that was almost tender. Nell found her eyes filling with tears. This was what she'd wanted so desperately, for herself and her baby. She had a home.

But where was Blake?

Blake was trying hard not to be there. Really hard. But there wasn't enough work.

Jason Gunner must be the only casualty in the whole of Sandy Ridge, he thought desperately as he stood at the nurses' station and wondered what to do next. The hospital was three-quarters empty. Every patient who possibly could had gone home. For those who remained there were the sounds of individual festivities as each family made a party around their special patient's bed.

These were private parties and he wasn't wanted.

Maybe he could go for a run now, he thought. After all, the beach would be deserted. But he knew he'd be seen—which meant Nell would be offended. To run in solitary state while the rest of the town ate their Christmas dinners would have everyone feeling sorry for him. People would be calling out for him to come and share their dinners, and the last thing he wanted was sympathy.

Why should he want it? His solitude was self-imposed. That was what he wanted. Wasn't it?

Nell would be carving the turkey by now.

What Nell was doing had nothing to do with him, he told himself fiercely. Nothing at all. He'd ring her to tell her he was busy, and then he'd go back to his own kitchen and eat.

His hand wouldn't quite lift the receiver.

OK. He'd eat and then ring, he decided. Then she'd think the medical need had been really urgent—something had happened that meant he hadn't even been able to phone.

But back at his apartment, his ham and the strawberries looked absolutely pathetic.

'Merry Christmas, Sutherland,' he muttered to himself as he stared at the plate of ham he'd cut from Ernest's bone, and he couldn't help thinking that even Ernest would be having a better Christmas than he was.

He was being pathetic. This was what he wanted! He opened a bottle of wine, took his ham and carried it into the living room. Here was Nell's tree, the only thing she'd left for him. His three haemorrhoid angels beamed from the tip, and their smiles mocked him. Fool, they said, and he knew they were right.

'I can't go.'

'You promised you would if you could.'

'So you were stupid. You're getting yourself into deep water, Blake Sutherland.' Heck, he was going barmy here, talking to himself and a bunch of paper angels, but there was no one else to talk to and his need to unburden his soul was overpowering.

'That's what you want.'

'It's not.'

'Well, you could just go out to her place and eat. After all, half your geriatric practice is there. Maybe it wouldn't hurt.'

Maybe.

Maybe he couldn't help himself. Maybe he was going mad, but with a groan he put the ham aside. Sensible or not, he was going to share Christmas with Nell.

Her back was on fire. As the meal continued Nell grew more and more aware of the pain. She'd been trying to ignore it all morning, and while there'd been things to do she'd managed, but now... She'd been on her feet too much, she told herself, and she shouldn't have carried the pudding. Now she was suffering the consequences.

Around her, the meal was everything she'd hoped. The food was fantastic and every person there was aching for a good time. With company like this, her party couldn't help but be a success.

Oh, but her back hurt.

Where was Blake?

He wasn't coming, she thought as the piles of Moreton Bay bugs and oyster shells were cleared and the turkey was carved—and by the time everyone's plates were heaped with the magnificent main course she was sure of it.

No matter. It didn't matter. These were her people and she didn't need anyone else. Hadn't she sworn that when she'd cut up her king-sized quilt?

It was just…her back hurt so much.

'Are you all right, girl?' Grace was looking at her with a strange expression on her face. 'You look…'

'Tired. I'm just a bit tired.' But the pain was like hot knives. Heck, she must have pulled something when she'd lifted the pudding, and she couldn't afford to be sick, she thought desperately. It'd spoil her guests' Christmas. Besides, she'd promised Blake two more weeks of medicine.

'Are you sure?' There was real concern on Grace's face, and Nell dredged up a smile.

'I'm fine. Honest.'

'You don't look fine. You look just how your—' She bit off her sentence, and if she hadn't been concentrating on her back Nell would have probed deeper.

'I'll get the gravy,' she said, realising the jug was still in the kitchen. It'd give her a blessed couple of minutes away to grimace in private, and maybe she could risk taking a painkiller.

'I'll get it.'

'No.' Nell put her hand on Grace's shoulder to stop her rising and she used the hold to lever herself to her feet. She felt somehow extraordinarily heavy. Extraordinarily…

No! Realisation came with her first major contraction. Her waters burst right as the knowledge slammed home. She doubled over with pain, and she cried out with the shock of it. And a dozen of Sandy Ridge's geriatrics were left open-mouthed as their hostess buckled to her knees and stayed there.

CHAPTER ELEVEN

BLAKE walked up the verandah steps, wondering what on earth he was doing. His last two Christmases he'd spent alone. He was accustomed to it. It didn't matter. The celebrations were way out of scale anyway, he thought. Gross commercialisation. He didn't need it.

But his legs kept carrying him forward. Nell's face, disappointed but stoic, was before him. He'd promised. She didn't think he'd come, he knew, and suddenly he wanted to see her face when he walked into the room. Because he knew it'd light up, and those gorgeous green eyes would smile a welcome and she'd make room for him by...

He was being a romantic fool! But his step quickened, nevertheless, and by the time the front door was flung wide he was almost running.

And so was Ethel. She burst out of the front door like a cannonball and when she saw Blake she almost fell into his arms—which was quite something as she weighed twenty stone.

Blake gasped and caught her—sort of—and she looked at him as though she couldn't believe he was really there.

'Oh, Dr Sutherland.' She was so desperate she could hardly get the words out. 'The phone's not on here yet, and I was just running next door to phone you.'

'I said I'd come.' Surely there had been no need for such urgency.

But it seemed there was. 'Come quick.' She hauled herself out of his grasp and grabbed his arm, dragging him into the hall. 'Quick. Dr McKenzie's having her baby on the dining-room floor.'

*   *   *

It wasn't quite as bad as that.

By the time he reached her, they'd carried Nell into the main bedroom and laid her on her grandparents' big bed. Now she lay wide-eyed with fright, gripping Grace's hand like she was drowning, and when Blake pushed his way through the crowd around the bed she gave a sob of sheer terror and clutched him, too.

'It's coming. Blake, my baby's coming, and it can't. I'm only thirty-four weeks. It'll die. Blake, stop it. I need a salbutamol drip. I need… Dear God, I don't know what I need. Oh…' Her voice tailed into a moan as the next contraction hit.

'Can someone fetch my bag?' Blake tossed his car keys to where at least eight senior citizens crowded around him. Grace seemed the most competent of the lot of them, and the most concerned. 'Grace, can you stay?' He glanced at the sea of elderly faces, each capped with a gay Christmas hat and each looking equally worried and agog. 'Everyone else, I suggest you finish your Christmas dinner while you wait for news of what's happening. I'm sure that's what Dr McKenzie wants.'

What Dr McKenzie wanted didn't include a baby, but that was exactly what she was getting. Blake did a swift examination and all it told him was that they were far too late to get her to the hospital. They were too late for anything but delivery.

'How sure are you of your dates?' he demanded, cutting through Nell's mist of pain and fear with his curt command.

Nell caught her breath on a sob and tried to make herself think. 'I'm…I'm sure.'

'Why are you sure?'

'I dated it from last menstruation.'

'You had a normal period?'

'I don't know. I guess.' She was panting with effort, and a sheen of sweat covered her forehead. 'I must have. It *was* a period. Richard and I were arguing. Maybe…'

Maybe if she'd been emotionally upset she wouldn'
have noticed if it had been much lighter than usual!

'You didn't have an ultrasound.'

'No, I…' She bit her lip on pain. 'It was all such a mess
I didn't.'

'So you're not absolutely sure.'

'I must be.' It was a wail. Another contraction rolled
through, and Blake winced. They were less than a minute
apart—and the head was crowning already!

'OK, Grace, we need lots of hot soapy water and as many
towels as you can find. Can you ask Ethel if she can use
my car phone to ring the hospital? Tell the nurses what's
happening, ask them to send a midwife and tell them to put
the Blairglen neonatal team on standby.'

In the face of this crisis Grace was swift and incisive,
dropping her years like magic. 'You want them to come at
once?'

'The midwife, yes, but the neonatal team, no.' The
Blairglen neonatal team flew anywhere in the district to
take premature babies back to the city for specialist attention, but… 'I'm not convinced this is early.'

'It's early.' Nell almost yelled. 'It's six weeks early.
Blake, stop it.'

'If I stop it now you'll have a baby half in and half out,'
Blake told her, and he grinned. 'You've learned breathing
techniques?'

'No. Yes. Ow…'

'Breathe, Nell,' he told her. 'Concentrate.'

'I don't want to concentrate. I don't want a baby.'

'You know, I'm very sure you do.' He took her hand,
and forced her terrified gaze to meet his. For a moment,
mid-contraction, he had her complete attention. 'Nell, by
the look of it you're having a normal delivery and a normal
baby. That's what you want, isn't it?'

'I… Yes. Oh, Blake…'

'Then what are we waiting for?' he asked. 'To have your
baby in your own home, with all your friends… And on

Christmas Day to boot.' He waited until the next contrac-tion came through and his hands held hers all the time, imparting strength.

'OK, Nell,' he told her softly, but there was still strength behind the words. 'You have me and you have Grace. And we both love you and won't let anything happen—to you or your baby. Do you trust us?'

Her attention was caught. She looked up into his eyes and took a searing breath, and he felt her body relax. He felt the terror dissipate. Resolution came to take its place. 'Yes…' It was a breathless whisper but it was enough, and Blake's smile encompassed her as a great hug might have.

'OK, Dr McKenzie, I believe we'll try for the full catas-trophe. Grace let's go for it. Nell, I'm afraid the time for talking is past. Shut up and push.'

'Why should I shut up?' It was a hint of the old Nell, belligerent and bossy. 'Why should you—?'

The next contraction hit.

She shut up and pushed.

And ten minutes later, before any nurse could arrive and before any more preparations could be made other than boiling water and warming towels, Blake lifted a tiny bun-dle of baby away from his mother.

Swiftly he cut the cord, checked the baby and discovered a perfect, near full-term baby boy. For some reason he was close to tears. Why, for heaven's sake? He'd delivered babies before. But he'd never delivered Nell's.

Forcing himself to be practical, he wrapped the infant in a warmed towel and handed him to Grace. After coping with the afterbirth, he washed his hands in some of the gallons of hot water—good grief, the back-up team had boiled enough to bathe an elephant—and then he moved to Nell's head, gripped her hands and held hard.

As the baby had cannonballed its way into the world, Nell had slumped back, exhausted beyond belief. Now her eyes had closed. The baby had arrived like a steam train

and Nell was bordering on shock. Not many first babies
arrived as hard and as fast as this one, and the shock to
Nell's body must be massive.

He needed to set up a drip. She could use some fluid.
But first…

'Nell?' It was a whisper. He lifted her wrist to find her
pulse steady and strong, and he felt better for it. 'Nell,' he
said again, and this time it was a command.

She opened her eyes, but they were full of fear. Full of
pain. She was bracing herself for the worst. 'Oh, Blake.
Oh, dear God…' Her voice cracked on a sob. 'Is it…is my
baby dead?'

'Give her the baby, Grace,' Blake said, and Grace smiled
her joy. She came forward, knelt by the bedside and held
out the tiny, warmly wrapped bundle for his mother to see.

'Look, Nell,' Blake ordered softly. 'See your son.'

And he was just perfect. He had huge eyes, just like his
mother's, already wide and wondering, and showing not a
hint of distress. And he had a mass of burnt red hair—just
like Nell's.

And just like…Grace's?

Grace's eyes were swimming with tears, and Blake
grinned. This felt good. It felt right, and more and more he
figured what he suspected was possible.

'He's a perfect baby boy,' he told Nell, and he stroked
a finger across her cheek to collect a teardrop. 'Just perfect.
Ten fingers. Ten toes. Everything. I'd say he might be a
week or two early, but certainly no more. And I'd guess
he's about six pounds. He's small enough so you haven't
even torn. So…'

The temptation to stroke her cheek again was irresistible,
and he did just that. 'Perfect,' he whispered, and maybe he
wasn't just talking about the baby. But somehow he hauled
himself back on track. 'A perfect little boy. What are you
going to call him?'

'What…?' Nell was so dazed she could hardly speak.
Grace manoeuvred the bundle into her waiting arms, and

Nell held him close and gazed down at her baby in awe. 'Oh,' she said on a sigh of discovery. 'He looks like…'

'He looks like his mother,' Blake said, and grinned. A perfect birth—a perfect baby—meant doctors were superfluous. He was superfluous. But he didn't feel superfluous. He felt fantastic! 'He looks like you. And…' He cast an odd glance up at Grace, but he was still sure he was right, and more and more this seemed the right time to tell her. 'And he also looks like your grandmother.'

'My grandmother.' Nell was exploring every last feature of her little son's face, and she was awed and wondrous. 'Oh… You knew my grandmother. But he doesn't look like her.' Her brow furrowed, unable to make the connection.

There wasn't one. 'I don't mean your grandmother who died,' Blake told her, and it was too much. Hell, both women were close to tears, and here he was ready to join them. He knew this was none of his business but he was going to do it anyway. 'I mean your living grandmother. The lady who's just given you your son.'

'My grandmother…' Nell was so confused that she cuddled her son for about five minutes before speaking again. Grace and Blake were content to wait. And watch. After one startled glance, Grace had opened her mouth and shut it again, leaving it to Nell to figure things out. Finally she thought it through and tried again. 'Grace…' Nell's eyes lifted to the elderly woman by the bed. 'You mean Grace is my grandmother?'

'I mean Grace, and I'm right, aren't I, Grace?' Blake demanded. When the old lady couldn't speak he drew her to sit on the bed beside him. Grace was weeping openly now, tears forming rivulets down her weather-worn cheeks. 'Nell, Grace is certainly your grandmother. Your mother loved Grace's son, Michael. Michael died before they could be married, but you're the result.' He smiled and looked down at the wrapped baby in Nell's arms. 'So this little boy is Grace's great-grandson.'

'But…how did…how did you know?' Grace seemed almost as confused as Nell. Almost as shocked.

'I guessed,' Blake told her. 'I knew something had happened to your Mike, and when your husband was dying he told me that Mike had got a girl into trouble. He told me Mike wanted to marry her but the girl's parents wouldn't hear of it. They sent the girl away to stay with her aunt and they wouldn't give Mike her address. She came back, though. When Nell was three months old she returned. Mike would have married her in all honour—even though they were just kids, they were desperately in love, and you both supported him, but he was drowned just before she came back. So Nell's mother returned to nothing—just her parents' awful judgement.'

'Oh, Nell…'

'You wanted to keep the baby, but Nell's parents told you that you'd already destroyed her mother's life with your kindness. They denied the baby was Mike's, and they locked you out.'

'We wanted so much…' It was a thready, broken whisper, but Grace was looking straight at Nell. 'So much… Nell, your mother was such a lovely girl. Just like you. Laughing. Happy. Despite her awful parents. She was like a daughter to us, so much so that we didn't realise until too late that she and Mike… I mean, we'd thought of them as almost brother and sister…'

'And you never told Nell.'

Still Grace was talking to Nell, her voice a shamed whisper. 'We couldn't. We knew there'd be a riot if we told you when you were a child, and then you left. And when you came back I was too ashamed. I should have made a bigger push to keep you. But our loving your mother destroyed her, so we couldn't do…we couldn't do the same to you.'

'You don't destroy someone by loving them.' Blake couldn't help himself. His chest had expanded by about six notches and he felt like having a weep himself. 'Nell, your nether regions are looking great. Your baby's looking great. Your grandmother's looking great. How's that for an instant family? What more do you want?'

And Nell looked up at him in wonder. So much had happened so fast. He'd given her the world. Her baby. Her grandmother. It was wrong to want more. But...

'I want *you*,' she whispered.

And then, as he stood stupidly by her bedside, she managed a smile, albeit a shaky one.

'I love you, Blake Sutherland,' she told him, and her voice was sure and strong, a declaration for the world as well as for herself. 'And I'll love you for ever.' She smiled and smiled, her eyes misty with tears of joy, and she held her baby close. 'You're right. You don't destroy someone by loving them. How can you? You can only give and give, and hope and hope. Like I'm hoping now.'

But, despite her joy, her eyelids were drooping with exhaustion. 'Go and eat your Christmas dinner,' she ordered them both. 'Because my son and I intend to sleep.'

It was a riot of a Christmas dinner. Blake and Grace emerged to cheers all round and tears and hugs, and you would have thought it was Blake who was the father the way this crazy lot of elderly folk reacted.

And he didn't mind at all. He felt... He felt terrific! For some reason he felt like a vast weight had been lifted from his shoulders, a weight he hadn't known he'd been carrying.

'I want *you*.'

The words drifted over and over in his mind—in his heart—and he barely heard what everyone else was saying.

'I want you.'

Then Ethel carried in the pudding—and what a pudding! It was the mother and father of all puddings. They'd flamed it, and two of the old men carried it from the kitchen as a ball of blue-gold fire. He'd be treating them for burns next, he thought. Ralph had Parkinson's disease, for heaven's sake—he normally shook all over—and here he was bearing flame, but he didn't even look like dropping it.

They put it in front of Blake. 'You do the honours, Doc,' they told him. 'Doc McKenzie should be doing it but she's got herself otherwise occupied.'

So he sliced the pudding and loaded his portion with brandy sauce and whipped cream and ice cream—and then a bit more brandy sauce for good measure. And then a bit more, because he felt just fine.

Finally they were gone. The table was cleared, the refrigerator stocked with enough leftovers to last for days, the washing-up had been done and the town's elderly folk, Wendy, Jason, Kyle and Christy made their way shakily home.

Jason was back on his bike but the rest of them were walking, which was just as well, given the amount of brandy sauce consumed. Only Grace remained, settling herself on the porch swing and smiling and smiling, like all her Christmases had come at once. Nell was her family—her grandchild—and her time for claiming her had come, but she was willing and wanting to share.

'She should be stirring,' she told Blake, looking at her watch. 'It's about four hours…'

'She might sleep around the clock.'

But Grace wanted a happy ending here, and she wanted it fast. The writing was on the wall, but if Blake was allowed to leave… He'd haul himself back into his shell, she thought, and it might take Nell months to get him out again. Grace had the greatest confidence in her granddaughter, but if she could help, then she would.

'I'm sure you should check her obs,' Grace said to Blake, and she grinned. 'I started nurse training once, you know, before I decided I was born to be a fisherwoman, and I remember that patients weren't allowed to sleep for more than four hours. They might get the idea that the medical staff weren't necessary—and that would never do, now, would it?'

'No, indeed.' Blake sounded bemused. He'd sounded bemused since he'd delivered the baby, Grace thought, and she was pleased by it. He was nicely off balance and she intended that he stay that way.

'And it'd be even worse if *Nell* found that you were unnecessary.'

'Grace…'

'Go in to her,' Grace told him, and gave him a push bedroom-wards. 'And, for heaven's sake, do what you want to do. It's time you looked out for yourself for a change. Give the girl what she wants most for Christmas—and get yourself what you want most into the bargain.'

'I don't—'

'You do, you know,' she said wisely. 'Now, go.'

He did. Blake paused at the bedroom door and he looked across at the great bed where Nell was sleeping and he felt his heart lurch within his chest. She was curled up like a kitten.

Or maybe not a kitten, he thought as he watched her. Maybe she was more like a fiercely protective mother cat, her arms curled around her bundle of baby and her face resting against the soft fleece of her baby son's wrapping.

She'd had such a hard time… Her short-cropped curls were clinging damply to her face. Her skin was far too pale, and her freckles stood out far too clearly. She looked about ten!

No! A surge of longing so fierce rose inside him that it threatened to overwhelm him. She wasn't about ten, he thought savagely. She was a grown woman—she was every inch a woman—and she was so desirable…

He felt his hands clenching into fists, and his nails were digging into his palms. Dear God…

Nell opened her eyes and she smiled, and as she did so, knowledge slammed home like a thunderbolt. He'd been so afraid of exposing himself to pain again—of loving as he'd loved Sylvia. But this wasn't like that. It wasn't in the least like that. This wasn't a love that exposed one to pain. It was no bitter-sweet barb, waiting to hurt him and waiting to hurt others with it.

It was a different sort of loving—the right sort. It was infinitely precious, infinitely tender and infinitely wonderful. It was love as he'd never loved in his life before.

'Nell…' And all the joy of the day was in his voice. After all, it was Christmas. The time of giving.

He'd already given, he thought dazedly. His heart was hers. It was just up to Nell to accept.

'You said… You said you wanted me,' he managed in a voice that was so unsteady he could hardly comprehend it was his.

'Did I?' Her eyes were wary.

'Yes.'

'You can never depend on what a woman says in labour.'

'So you don't want me.'

'I never said that.'

Hmm.

'Are you hungry?' he asked, and he smiled at her. And such a smile… It was all Nell could do not to gasp.

'Um…maybe.'

'There's Christmas pudding and brandy sauce.'

'How about if I just have brandy sauce?'

'You can have anything you damned well want.'

'Including you?'

That set him back. He stared and she smiled across at him, but her eyes were suddenly unsure. 'I guess,' he said. 'Nell…'

'You gave me my grandmother,' she said softly. 'And my son.'

'You know where the brandy sauce recipe came from?' he asked, because the tension was unbearable and he had to break it somehow. 'From Grace. We figured out what had happened. Your mother used to sneak over to visit them on Christmas Day and she wrote down the recipe. It's like a final piece of evidence.'

'I don't need evidence to know I'm Grace's granddaughter,' Nell said softly, but her eyes were still on his face and her attention was only half on what she was saying. The rest was devouring the way Blake was looking at her. 'I guess from the time I came back to town, I sensed that I was loved.'

'By Grace.'

'Who else would love me?' But her voice was strained, and he couldn't bear it. Not now. Not when the joy of the world was in his heart.

'I would.'

Silence. 'Blake, you don't have to. Just because I...'

Still he didn't move. 'Just because you what?'

And in the end it was easy. 'Just because I love you,' she whispered, and the whole world held its breath.

And that was enough for him. He was across the room in seconds, stooping and gathering her into the safety of his arms, her tiny son cocooned between them both. 'Nell. My love...'

And then there was no need for words. He was kissing her and kissing her, tenderly at first, wondering, but then more urgently, his kiss a claim and a giving all on its own.

'My Nell...' Finally he broke away—an inch, but no more. Just enough to get the words out.

'You can't...' She gazed up into his eyes, and her whole body trembled.

'What can't I do?'

'You can't love me.'

'Watch me.'

'But I'm your Christmas present.'

'So?'

'I'm only yours for four weeks.' But she was smiling now as he put her away from him and held her at arm's length, and the trembling had ceased. What she read in his face was fine by her.

'When I was two,' he said softly, smiling and smiling, 'I was given a fire engine for Christmas. It was a particularly splendid fire engine.'

'So?' She was smiling so much she could hardly speak. Between them lay her tiny son, just hours old, and Blake looked down at him and his smile encompassed him as well. Answering an unspoken question.

'I'm thirty-four years old,' Blake said softly. 'I've kept my fire engine for thirty-two years and it's still going strong. I might get it out and play with it this very night just to check it's still in working order for one young man who might have a use for it someday.'

'I don't understand,' Nell whispered, but she did and her heart was singing.

'It's simply that I keep my Christmas presents for a very long time,' he told her, and his hands held her and his eyes caressed her face. 'Thirty-two years for my fire engine is the record, but I'm working on it. I reckon fifty's a better bet. What do you say, Nell McKenzie? Will you be my Christmas present for fifty years?'

'Fifty years!'

'What's wrong with fifty years?'

'Just that it's not nearly enough,' she said strongly, and she put her hand around his head and found his mouth with her lips. 'Oh, Blake, my darling, merry Christmas. For now and for ever.'

CHAPTER TWELVE

'NOT again?' Blake groaned as he opened the door. 'Jason Gunner, you did this to us last Christmas.'

'Last Christmas was the bike.' Jason stood on the front porch and grinned, blood dripping from a very impressive cut on his elbow. 'This year we got a trampoline.'

Blake sighed as Nell emerged from the kitchen to see what was happening. One very small boy crawled determinedly behind her—where his mum went, Michael went—and Ernest brought up the rear. 'Nell, look what we have here. It's Jason.'

'Well, I'm not stitching you on the bathroom floor,' Nell said sternly. 'Look what happened when we did it last year.'

'Hey, you're only four months pregnant this time.'

'It's pregnant enough not to take any chances,' Nell told them. 'Take him into the kitchen. I'll move the turkey from the table.'

'I'll move the turkey,' Blake growled, but he was caressing his wife with his eyes. 'You're right. We're taking no chances.'

'If I can lift Michael then I can lift a turkey.' Nell hoisted her one-year-old into her arms and hugged him. 'And you'd best hurry. With a birthday and Christmas on the one day, we have a heap of celebrating to do.'

'Let me take him.' Grace came through from the kitchen, wiping flour from her hands. She took her great-grandson into her arms and held him close, their copper heads blending together as she planted a kiss on his grubby cheek. 'Michael Blake Sutherland, what have you been up to?'

'He's had his fire engine in the sand pit,' Blake told her, and Nell smiled fondly at the pair of them.

'You realise nothing Santa can give him this Christmas can ever come up to the standard of your thirty-three-year-old Christmas present. Your fire engine's the best.'

'No,' Blake told her, and his arm came around his wife's waist and hugged hard. 'It's not the best Christmas present. Last year I received a wife and a son. What could be better than that?'

'A trampoline,' Jason said promptly, and glared at them both. 'Aren't you going to fix my elbow? I'm dripping.'

'So you are.' Blake grinned. 'If I didn't know you'd deserved it, I'd be worried. But come along.' He steered the nine-year-old kitchenwards. 'Let's get this turkey off the table and you on it.'

'Hey, I haven't started the brandy sauce yet,' Grace called as both doctors disappeared toward the kitchen. 'You be quick.'

'We'll be the fastest stitchers in the West,' Blake called back. 'If brandy sauce is at stake… How many eggs are we putting in this year?'

'A dozen.'

'It's not nearly enough.' And as he reached the kitchen door he paused, his arm around his wife. Both of them looked back at Grace and they smiled.

'Our family's extended, and then some,' Blake told Michael's great-grandmother. 'I want enough brandy sauce to feed all Sandy Ridge and a few more besides.'

'How many have you invited?' Nell asked, startled.

'Twelve for Christmas dinner, but afterwards…'

'Afterwards?'

'Afterwards everyone who loves us will be here to sing carols. So we need to be ready.'

'Everyone who loves us?' Nell grinned up into her husband's face. 'Oh, for heaven's sake, Blake Sutherland, stop looking smug. You look like the cat that got the canary.'

'I'm not. I'm the Blake that got Nell.'

He stooped, and she succumbed to his kiss for an instant and then pushed him away, laughing. 'Blake, Jason's waiting. Blake, you can't kiss me like that in front of the children. Blake!'

'Well, you will wear those overalls and you know they always do things to my insides. And, besides, that's what you get for hanging mistletoe.'

'There's no mistletoe here.'

'Mistletoe's somewhere and mistletoe's infectious,' Blake said softly, cupping his wife's hands in his palms and stooping towards her once again. 'As a medical condition, I'd say it's extremely infectious and it lasts a very long time. Fifty years or more. As diseases go, it takes the cake.'

'There's no cure?'

'Just brandy sauce to keep it fed,' he said softly. 'And a baby or two. And you. Who could ask for more than that, my love?'

'Hey, remember me,' Jason said indignantly, and Blake grinned and waved his hand at the boy.

'Join the queue,' he told him. 'This doctor's busy. He's dealing with a very urgent Christmas present—in fact, it's so urgent it's left over from last year. And he always treats emergency cases first.'

'Always?' Nell whispered as Blake's lips claimed hers once again.

'Always.'

For ever.

'Nell, shall we give them our recipe?'

'But it's a family secret.'

'They *have* just read our story and it *is* Christmas. The time of sharing.'

'And I guess we've so much to share. Grace and Michael and you and me—and our own special Ernest and a new little life on the way. You've talked me into it, my love. So...Merry Christmas, everyone. From Blake and from Grace and from Ernest and from me. With love.'

BRANDY SAUCE

1 egg, separated
120 g / 4 oz / ³/₄ cup sifted icing sugar
125 ml / 4 fl. oz / ¹/₂ cup whipped cream
45 ml / 3 tablespoons brandy

Beat egg white until stiff. Gradually add icing sugar, a tablespoon at a time. Fold in whipped cream and beaten egg yolk. Flavour with brandy to taste. Chill.

Multiply the recipe as many times as you like.

Enjoy!

Modern Romance™
...seduction and
passion guaranteed

Tender Romance™
...love affairs that
last a lifetime

Sensual Romance™
...sassy, sexy and
seductive

Blaze
...sultry days and
steamy nights

Medical Romance™
...medical drama on
the pulse

Historical Romance™
...rich, vivid and
passionate

27 new titles every month.

*With all kinds of Romance for
every kind of mood...*

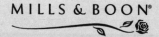

MILLS & BOON®

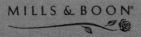

Don't miss *Book Five* of this BRAND-NEW 12 book collection 'Bachelor Auction'.

Who says money can't buy love?

On sale 3rd January

Available at most branches of WH Smith, Tesco, Martins, Borders, Eason, Sainsbury's, and all good paperback bookshops.

BA/RTL/5

FREE
2 BOOKS
AND A SURPRISE GIFT!

We would like to take this opportunity to thank you for reading this Mills & Boon® book by offering you the chance to take TWO more specially selected titles from the Medical Romance™ series absolutely FREE! We're also making this offer to introduce you to the benefits of the Reader Service™ —

- ★ FREE home delivery
- ★ FREE monthly Newsletter
- ★ FREE gifts and competitions
- ★ Exclusive Reader Service discount
- ★ Books available before they're in the shops

Accepting these FREE books and gift places you under no obligation to buy; you may cancel at any time, even after receiving your free shipment. Simply complete your details below and return the entire page to the address below. **You don't even need a stamp!**

YES! Please send me 2 free Medical Romance books and a surprise gift. I understand that unless you hear from me, I will receive 4 superb new titles every month for just £2.55 each, postage and packing free. I am under no obligation to purchase any books and may cancel my subscription at any time. The free books and gift will be mine to keep in any case.

M2ZEC

Ms/Mrs/Miss/Mr ....Initials ....

BLOCK CAPITALS PLEASE

Surname ....

Address ....

....

....Postcode ....

Send this whole page to:
UK: FREEPOST CN81, Croydon, CR9 3WZ
EIRE: PO Box 4546, Kilcock, County Kildare (stamp required)